Are You There, God?

ARE YOU THERE, GOD?

by
Jane Brewington

Beacon Hill Press of Kansas City
Kansas City, Missouri

Copyright, 1975
Beacon Hill Press of Kansas City

ISBN: 0-8341-0358-3

Printed in the
United States of America

Dedication

to
my dearly beloved family—
Mom, Dad, Robert, and Irma.
They are my greatest blessing.

Contents

Contents

Foreword

When the manuscript for Miss Brewington's book arrived, it was passed from office to office as though it were a just-published best seller. There were "rave" reviews by many, who said this one not only had to be published, but it must be assured a wide distribution. There is a reason. Miss Brewington has communicated what so many of us have tried to express, but she has done it most eloquently and effectively.

Her message will reach 10,000 college-age young people, as the Departments of World Missions, Home Missions, Youth, and Church Schools all expressed unanimous desire to sponsor the book for distribution to every student in our American and Canadian Nazarene colleges. A part of the fall, 1975, Youth in Mission Festivals will be the sharing of Miss Brewington's testimony as presented in the following pages.

Because those responsible for the missionary reading program are convinced many of our people will feel left out, a decision has been made to include *Are You There, God?* as a part of the 1976-77 book list. I predict an enthusiastic response from all age levels. In fact, I think it is very possible that this one will indeed become a missionary best seller.

JERALD D. JOHNSON
Executive Secretary,
Department of World Missions

1

Finding a Navigator

All right. So maybe you don't consider 26 to be all that venerable. But let me tell you—it all depends on your point of view. It is common knowledge that 26 and married is just off the starting block, but 26 and single is over the hill. Or at least the compassionate-looking world seems to tell me this. I have a few thoughts of my own on that subject and on quite a few other areas, as a matter of fact. So I might as well speak my mind.

* * *

They were nothing too extraordinary—my first few years in this world. Just your average little kid growing up in your average big city. I did have a childhood sweetheart, one who promised fair and square at the ripe old age of six that he would marry me—but, alas, here I am. Funny about first loves, puppy though they be. Nobody forgets who it was or when. And when finished, it's the one "love" that can be remembered with a smile.

Detroit, my entry point in this world, was quite the city with plenty of hustle and bustle—except, that is, on Sundays. Even then, for a youngster there were potentially some things to do. But while Sunday afternoons may herald delightful possibilities for the young, they have a strange lulling effect on the old, producing the almost international institution of the Sunday afternoon nap. Some things are never understood, and children will just never understand Mom's and Dad's Sunday post-meal naps. I sure didn't. But with five or so hours of the day filled with various church services I managed to fight off the phantom of boredom. Having Walt Disney on Sunday nights at the same time as church, however, was about the toughest cross I bore those days, and I felt persecuted plus.

One day I realized that the sturdy pillars of my foundation were beginning to sway beneath me. "Why does Dad's being laid off mean we have to move halfway around the world? We have to eat? Well, we'll grow some tomatoes in the backyard or something. We just can't go off and leave everything I know and understand. California? It's a nice place to visit, but I wouldn't want to live there."

Want to guess what happened? At the ripe old age of 10 years, I migrated with my family to Coalinga, Calif. Lost in a world with no familiar landmarks, I was completely unimpressed by the signs on the highway that mocked my young presence. "Go West, young man, go West." All I wanted was to go back home.

It's a bit difficult to explain Coalinga appropriately to you. It's the kind of town that when people ask you where you're from, you oblige by telling them, but immediately throw in some directions or names of large neighboring cities. That's to ward off the certain question, "Where's that, anyway?" Unfortunately, Coalinga isn't really near much of anything but some barren hills. Dry as a desert and lacking any particular distinction or atmosphere, I really thought we had moved to nowhere.

The fact that 110° was *not* the record high for the summer did nothing to comfort my weary bones. I felt like Gretel about to climb into the witch's oven, but I could figure no fancy footwork to get out of my situation. One day I would realize those brown hills could look like velvet and the heat serve only to enhance the dip in the school pool, but that kind of appreciation only comes with familiarity and familiarity takes time. Fortunately, or unfortunately, depending on which side of the calendar one stands, I had plenty of time. For a dozen years Coalinga was home.

The greatest single blow I felt in Coalinga was in the size of the local church, or rather its lack of size. "You can come out now, the game is over. Where is everybody? What do you mean, this *is* everybody? Man alive, don't you people ever sing 'Bringing in the Sheaves'?" After being in the big city, the Coalinga Church of the Nazarene introduced a whole new chapter in my life. The church had always had a definite place in our family. We each had held down our own roles: Dad remodeled, Mother taught, my sister Irma played the piano, and I got in the way. But even at that, we were just part of a huge co-op of friends who came together in the common meetinghouse of our church.

But in Coalinga, we could count on being nearly a quarter of the congregation! Having previously experienced an abundant peer group, I now found hard pickings. Plus or minus a few, depending on the year, the size of my immediate age-group was suddenly pretty limited. Sometimes it was just me—all alone. And that's not very good company for a young person. When I would think about it —missing Walt Disney and having no one to scribble notes to either—it was almost more than I could bear.

However, I had amazingly little time to think about it. If we all had our jobs in Detroit, we all had our three dozen jobs in Coalinga. You weren't even allowed to mumble if only two or three jobs came your way. No, it just wouldn't do. Some (my mother included) applied themselves to more fronts than your average army would ever find wont to. At election time, everyone resigned his jobs—and then got talked back into them. There just really were not any other people to do them. But while we chafed pretty much at the time, I look back to those years with basically only one sentiment, that of great thankfulness.

Such a tiny little church! But a better preparatory school one never had. Any other place I would have stood back and watched and learned little, but not here. I had my fingers in every kettle. Most of the time I performed quite poorly, having no real precedent to follow. But I've often thought of Edison's adage, "A thousand mistakes makes an education of sorts." Ranked by mistakes, I surely came out *cum laude*. I know an awful lot of ways of how not to do things: how not to keep a four-year-old's attention with a story, how not to send used clothes to Chile, how not to transpose music, and so on. It would have been terribly defeating but for one thing. I was secure there—I was loved. Funny, like the song by Joni Mitchell, "Don't it always seem to be, that you don't know what you've got till it's gone?"[1]

There is one other aspect I should mention from that period of time if you are really going to understand the *me* of today. It seems all of my life I have moved, and then moved, and then moved again. Not always state to state or even town to town. In Coalinga alone I lived in seven different houses. No, Dad's not a preacher . . . no, not in the army . . . no, not bitten with the wanderlust. Sometimes in life it just works out that way. I calculate over my entire lifetime, to this date at any rate, I have called about 19 different places my home and I have visited many more. There were different reasons for moving most times, and

1. "Big Yellow Taxi," copyright 1970, Siquomb Publishing Corp., New York, N.Y.

they weren't bad or wrong reasons; they were just numerous. It has, however, had some telling effects on my life.

*   *   *

My story really begins with the call to higher education and my maiden flight from the nest. Suddenly I was no longer a nameless part of a larger unit. I was me, or at least so I thought at the time. Now I know *that me* waits out there in the future somewhere, but *that* was the beginning of *becoming*. My family had laid all the foundation stones they could for me: love, trust, discipline, prayer. And God seemed already to have some blueprints in hand about what He wanted constructed on that foundation. But the building would depend on me. You know, it's an awful responsibility to grow up.

The fact that I ever arrived at Pasadena College is the beginning of a very fascinating and continuing tale to me. Even if it weren't my own story, I think I would be interested, so let me continue. There's no way for me to get into this story, however, without my commencing to talk about God, which I suppose evokes one of three responses from you. You're either going to find some pleasure at that (perhaps because of your own past experiences) or you're going to feel nothing (also, I suppose, because of your own past experiences). Or, for perhaps the same reason, you're going to think, "Oh no, I was afraid of this."

Well, since I don't know the neighborhood your shoes have trod, I'm not going to argue the point, but seeing as how I've had some mighty interesting firsthand encounters with God that have kind of turned me upside down a few dozen times over, I think you should give me a chance. I mean if you stop reading now, I'll just feel like blubbering all over the place, and you know it's very sad to see old maids puddling the place up. So hang in there. Now, as I was about to say . . .

The fact that I was able to attend Pasadene College still amazes me since the school, as is usually the case, was not keen on trading an education for an IOU. Having just finished putting my sister through college, the old family budget was getting a bit arthritic and not at all eager to apply itself to another school year. So it was, during a period when the picture was financially grim, that I received a letter in the mail saying the state of California would like to foot my tuition for the next four years in any school I cared to choose. Now I always liked to think of myself as at least guardedly optimistic, but come on! When I applied for the scholarship, even my mother (typically motherly in affirming a belief that her daughter could do almost anything) had laughed at me for my silliness. And no, it wasn't a deprecating laugh; it was what would have to fall under the heading of realism. I had failed Spanish, and I sure wasn't prepared to brag about my physics and chemistry. In fact, there wasn't a whole lot to put forward as my best foot. I couldn't even be sure of an *A* in physical education. I was, for the most part, a middle-of-the-road student who wanted out of the central California desert.

Then how was it that this letter of glad tidings ever found its way to our house? Did anyone else apply? Yes, it seems they did. Was I better than they? No, I was not. Did some other factor intervene? No, but *Someone* did. "One isolated coincidence and you're going to try and convince me it was God?" No. That is what *I* think, but I won't try to convince you. I'll just tell the story and you can decide for yourself.

Now I suppose the most popular way of thinking of one's college days is with a certain sense of nostalgia. "Those were the days, my friends," as the song goes. Some songwriters can really speak to the heart, can't they? Well, that song spoke to about 50 percent of my days. The other 50 percent tended to repose under the influence of "Cry Me

16

a River." I figured it was just those adolescent years and time would march me out of those perplexing woods, but I've lost faith in that theory. I'm convinced the problems of life don't become any easier—they start hard and end hard. Certainly they vary, and what wreaks havoc in the life of an eight-year-old and what knocks Granny flat are completely differently shaped stumbling blocks. Nevertheless, they can all be categorized under the same general heading: Trials and Troubles. Any other viewpoint is going to end up putting you off center in your evaluation of your plight.

As crises go, there aren't really too many original ones on the market, although it kind of hurts for me to admit it. There is something wonderfully consoling in thinking that your particular situation is surely unique in its utter miserableness. I guess as long as you're set in your determination to spend some time wallowing in self-pity, the thought of a "private pool" adds that certain something that speaks of affluence. "Look at me. Here I am. Aren't I just exceptionally miserable?"

But most likely there have been, there are, and there will be other poor souls in the selfsame boat, going down the selfsame river of life. And strangely enough, your efforts expended in trying to steady their boat will often do amazing things for your own. Funny how one's own philosophy of survival can be quite seaworthy, but you often don't know how sensible it sounds until you try it out on someone else. And then, realizing it sounds pretty good, you think, Maybe I should try it out on myself.

But what of that first year of college? Well, I must admit that some rather sad times accompanied my realization that being in a place where you are surrounded by your own kind does not mean an instantly full calendar. In plain English that means I wasn't getting any dates. Ouch, that hurt! So much for the theory of availability. There were guys there, and they were my age. But despite it all, I plodded on toward old age alone. I made a lot of objections to the situation, but no one seemed to be listening.

College can be an awfully lonely place. It's fine for the beautiful people, for the ones who know how to go in and establish the relationships they seek, and for the ones who emotionally haven't gotten to the place that they crave anything more than their books. But for the hopeful, without any know-how or built-in advantages, it's a difficult proving ground.

At that tender age of innocence, I went even further to discover one of the greatest paradoxical tragedies that life has to offer. I fell in love with someone who had no love for me, while someone else fell for me—someone to whom I could manifest no love. As personal relationships go, there just isn't anything much sadder. Yes, all parties survived, but I'm not sure plain survival is always something to brag about. When I'm feeling a bit melancholy, I sometimes think back to the guy who thought so much of me. I think to myself, "He was a nice guy, maybe I should have married him. Then at least one of us would be happy." But when I give the subject a bit more thorough perusal, I know those are just so many words.

Now you may think it a bit impudent of me to do any philosophizing on marriage from the outside, looking in. But I figure a lot more analyzing may well take place out here in the cold than does within the cozy phenomena itself. We out here are always sifting the evidence in anticipation of arriving at the perfect conclusion for ourselves or are at least trying to justify our own "wise" dealings with these major issues in life—self-justification, in other words.

A successful marriage, it seems to me, must build upon a truly sound and stable foundation. There must be mutual interests, some shared background, some agreed-upon

18

priorities, goals, and love. Not that these things are immutable and can never change. But so that 15 years hence, when things are not as you had envisioned, and the wedding ties come again under close scrutiny, you can look back and know it was the right thing, and remember that the love that you felt then was a real and palpable thing.

In life you have good days and bad days that bring you to completely opposing conclusions. They can't both be true for they contradict. I have found it wisest to believe the good days. It was right then, it can be right now. Let's find that mutual ground and build again. Even without the *sensations* of the good day, the faith in what you had on that day can serve as an anchor in shifting seas. And to marry someone you're not really in love with is to deny yourself help in a future day when time has worn thin those ties that bind.

But lest we leave that first college year with a bad taste in our mouths, or even suggest that events all revolved around the boy/girl situation, I should now like to expose the other side of the coin. It wasn't really until I got into college that I became aware that the daily affairs of my life involved not just me, but my Creator. My busy Maker hadn't finished on August 4 (the day I was born) but was carrying right on as though He owned me or something! In fact, I was gaining the impression He had only just begun. In one way, I saw that as pretty fantastic. And surveying what I had accomplished thus far on my own, the potential of skilled help was pretty tantalizing. But in another light, I wasn't too sure that our final objectives were going to be the same and, frankly, I preferred my own road map rather than His.

I admit I had felt that God was talking to me about some full-time involvement, which, for a girl who liked nursing, I understandably figured meant being a missionary nurse. And while my body was willing, my spirit wasn't too sure. Things were fine as long as I remained young and naive enough to think of "orchid-encrusted jungles and paid travel tickets" every time someone mentioned missions. I could even identify some real compassion when starving children and perishing souls were mentioned.

But my enlightenment at college had also caused me to see a bit more of the reality of the missions scene. There really is not too much jungle left in the world, and even fewer come equipped with Tarzans. While there are still starving children in the world, most of them were not where I was likely to be sent, and, unfortunately, a lot of the perishing souls seemed quite content to perish—in fact, defiantly so. I learned that missions is not building a church, opening the doors, and watching the eager flood in. Missions is hard work, physically, spiritually, and emotionally. God goes with you, but how sad to get off the plane and find out the devil came as well.

All of that was complicated by the fact that I wasn't absolutely certain what God was asking me to do. I had read the story about Jonah often enough to know that if God really wanted me on the mission field, I might just as well pack my bags. But, on the other hand, I had no desire to go trooping into the fracas for the fun of it. As I got further and further into school, I knew I was going to have to decide. And I wanted to, because betwixt and between is a most unpleasant avenue on which to live one's life.

All told, I could think of only one good reason for my being a missionary: specifically, that God seemed to be pointing in that direction. I could think of innumerable good reasons why I should forget the whole thing, not the least of which was the fact that I was about as much like any missionary I had ever met as a frog looks like a prince, and I was pretty apprehensive about the possibility of any metamorphosis. Why couldn't I just be a happy, well-intentioned frog?

Arriving at the proverbial end of the rope one evening, I locked myself in my room and told the Lord I thought it was time I came to some conclusion on the matter. He seemed agreeable. So encouraged, I proceeded to wait for a final answer, filling any uncomfortable gaps of silence with one of the several fine points in my argument on why I should stay in my own lily pond.

I didn't get an answer—at least not for a while. All I could think about were a few scattered scriptures that seemed to talk about going. Fine, but I wanted to hear from God. It would take a few more years before I would really learn what true communication with God could mean. Meanwhile, it seemed things were a bit chancy. Knowing this, I was frightened deep down. I wanted to be sure. So as I sat there on the floor (one of my more favored places for serious thinking), I knew real misery.

In addition to not being sure, there was another factor that seemed to be weighing on my mind. I had almost worn a path in the carpet going to the altar about something holiness churches call sanctification. It was one great mystery to me. I had done everything anyone had ever told me to do, right down to the teary-eyed confession to a teacher that I had cheated on a test. But with all my seeking, I had to admit I still was an empty shell that night. Where had I gone wrong? What was a nice girl like me (that is the first use of one of my unfortunately more skilled arts of sarcasm) doing in a confused mess like this?

Well, I wasn't about to throw in the towel for another siege of indecision, so I persisted. I said, "Lord, from the time I was just a little girl You've been getting me ready for something, what with all that training in Coalinga, and those scriptures, and all those missionary messages that had my name on them." And He seemed to agree. "Now, why don't You tell me what I'm supposed to do? Tell me, and I'll do it." As I reflect back, it reminds me very much

21

of the Pharisees who, though they had seen Jesus perform countless miracles, wanted just one more. "Master, we would see a sign from thee."

One thing about God—He is awfully patient. At a point when anyone else would have been getting pretty uptight, God took it upon himself to explain the thing to me. It was my first big step; I didn't want to go wrong, understandably enough. And God didn't want me to go wrong either and for many years had patiently prepared me. The question now was, did I believe that God could communicate, prepare me for His job, bring me to a point of decision, and then abandon me to my own devices? No, that didn't add up. I was sure God wouldn't play games with me.

And I was also convinced, from someplace deep down inside, that God wanted me to be happy. He wasn't going to drag me off to the mission field as I clawed the ground and screamed, "I don't want to go, I don't want to go." The decision would have to be mine. I knew the Lord was there, and He was offering me something. It wasn't a way out that He had for me; it was courage.

I thought a long time and then addressed myself to my Architect. "Lord, I'm drawing a circle here and in that circle I'm putting all the things that I think are important to me: my future, my family, my potential." Silence. I continued, "Well, all right, I'm going to add the failures, the faults, and the *lack* of potential." Silence. "Okay, Lord, are You watching? I'm climbing into the circle too, Lord. I'm going to be a missionary unless You close every last, single door smack in my face and wedge them so they can't be pushed open. It's all I know to do, Lord." Silence. But not for very long.

Fantastic! Have you ever seen an old dormitory room start smiling and then laughing? Have you ever had the cool, fresh, clean taste of a strong mint permeate your whole being? Wow, what can I say? Did the Lord ever come that night! I had decided to trust God regardless of my feelings or lack of them. I believed that He would work it all out if I could muster the courage to shift out of neutral. Although seemingly blindfolded, I believed that when I needed to turn, He would be there to navigate my ship for me.

I see it now as my first awareness that God might well be able to fill a greater role in my life than just being the Addressee of my prayers. And He rewarded me with assurance—assurance *after* the fact. Suddenly I knew the Lord's will for my life, or at least as much as I needed to know at the time. And I knew that the Lord had accepted true claim on my life. I wasn't any longer really an *I*, I was a *We*. And it sure felt good!

2

On Starving to Death

This communication stuff can be pretty tricky, I find. No longer do we listen to our friends and accept what they say at face value. No, there is that other world—the world of hidden meaning. You *say* this, but you really *mean* that. I don't mean to be particularly critical of this phenomena, for frankly I find that it does seem to pan out as truth. But if you apply that theory to this book, you are going to end up in left field, when actually I'm headed for the right one. Since my college days and some royal blunders on my part in the area of communication, I have been working quite hard on saying what I mean. And while I've not found total success, I think it would be fair to say that what I'm saying in these pages you can take at face value.

College life is great, especially if it is in the hub of a big city and you're from the sticks. Disneyland was possible, Santa Monica beach reasonable, and Ernie Junior's Mexican restaurant practically next door! Unfortunately, though I would have liked to overlook it, there was also an academic side of college to cope with. And throughout my four years, there were some other hard facts that had to be faced. Placed in a formula it goes like this: School requires money, money comes from scholarships, scholarships are acquired by grades. No grades, no money, no school. Seeing as how I did make it through school, the assumption is that I applied myself, made the grades, and had the scholarships. Well, it wasn't quite that way.

Here is where you must begin to accept what I say at face value. I *did* study, but I was also trying to do odd jobs here and there to supplement what my parents were quite sacrificially sending me. Since I was carrying quite a large number of units, there was only so much time to go around. So I did what I could and waited for the results to come back. But somehow, while I was putting in three plus three, I was getting back nine. I would have been quite content with six and would have accepted three, but nine! There was obviously another factor involved causing this multiplication. I soon realized that's how math works when God does the figuring.

I'll stop with the fancy talk and tell you just what I mean. When I asked the Lord to help out with the studies, He took me a lot more literally than I ever expected. Things I didn't understand began to open up to me. On the tests I could study for my grades held up okay. But sometimes there just wasn't time to study properly, so I would just whisk through the book, randomly choose a few things to learn, and then flake out. (That's go to sleep for you on the other side of the generation gap.) On many occasions the Lord helped me as I took tests in this condition of preparation (if you can call it preparation).

One time, after having whispered a last "Please, Lord, help me," I turned the test over to find an amazing thing. Having learned 10 items out of a possible question list of 50 to 100 things and anticipating the worst, there appeared before me 10 questions on those 10 things I knew. Kind of leaves a person speechless! I got the highest grade in that class and probably did the least studying.

On another occasion, I somehow hadn't heard there

was even going to be a test and hadn't cracked the book yet on that particular subject. I came to class ignorant of the impending trauma. When the teacher said, "About the test today . . .," all I could think to say was, "O Lord," which was all that I could squeak, since my heart was in my mouth anyway. The teacher continued, "No reason, but I think we'll just put it off until tomorrow," as I melted into a grateful pool of sheer relief on the floor. Now the amazing thing is that I tell people this and no one really believes me. I have come through harder places since then (midwifery and Zulu, for example, which are both absolute puzzles for me).

When I try to tell people that I really didn't get myself through but God brought me out, no one seems convinced. People keep quoting this saying, "God helps those who help themselves." I'm sorry, but I can't buy that. My experience is that God helps those who *can't* help themselves. I'm not saying we shouldn't do our best, but what *God* does need have no relationship to what *we* do. I get keyed up when waiting for a big test, which is pretty bad news for me because I tend to employ the art of cramming at the last minute. On several occasions, where I had been relying on the fruits to be obtained from that last-minute endeavor, I arrived at the last minute to find I was too excited to study and finally had to abandon the effort for a few hours with my guitar and Bible.

But I *have* learned things and I *have* made the grades, and if you can take me at my word, you'll understand. God deserves the credit. I can be the only honest judge of that and, believe me, it's true. If you're wondering why all God's children don't hold scholarships, I can offer this thought: God wasn't polishing my ego; He had a plan for my life and He was working it out. For me, it seemed to require this "particular" kind of help. God has a plan for your life. If you truly want His will, He will work *His* plan out for you, whatever it may require. It's true—when God guides, God provides.

Having proved that theorem, I transferred to California State College at Los Angeles and the steadily increasing independence of an apartment. Probably I was a bit young. Definitely I was a bit naive when I made this transition to my new abode. But since Cal State had no real dormitories, my alternatives were limited. I thought I had lined up a roommate to share the place, but she decided it was a bit far removed from the gang in Pasadena and so moved back. I was going to be *so* brave! It was a "nice" little apartment—even if it was a bit old and decrepit. And the neighbors were such nice folks, so quiet, so peaceful!

Like I said—brother, was I naive! In the heart of Los Angeles, a few miles up from Watts, I was about to learn the realities of life. I figured that meant becoming reconciled to having to move half the living room furniture to pull my bed down from the wall each night, and then trying not to get lost in the valleys and gulleys I found in the mattress. There was, of course, my rather limited budget and the necessary reduction in the heat. But, considering myself the hardy type, I was game for that.

Gradually I began to see through my fog. The manager told me one day that my neighbor on the right had died quietly of natural causes. But I couldn't understand why the police had put sealing wax on the door and were going through so much investigation. "Yes, she and her husband did occasionally have a few loud words, but . . ." "What do you mean they weren't married?" Hmmm . . .

Then one evening the neighbors on the left, who I was beginning to think also might not have made it down the aisle, began getting a bit violent. Becoming somewhat accustomed to such, I didn't think too much about it until it began to sound as though the guy was getting the best of

27

the girl. Not liking to hear women getting slugged, I went to the phone to call the police. Just then I heard her wallop the guy so hard with something he hit our mutual wall with a thud. I put the phone down, thinking, Sounds like a fair fight after all. That certainly quieted things down, and soon apparently they had made up. My new neighbor on the right was a nice chap . . . when he was sober.

I felt quite safe in my apartment and quite safe in my car. Getting from the one to the other sometimes was a bit of a thriller. I remember manually closing the little elevator door while simultaneously pushing the third-floor button one evening with the oiled efficiency only the Lord can give, just exactly as my two cheery drunk pursuers reached their hands out to the elevator door. But it wouldn't open —I was gone. And once I somehow forgot and left my door unlocked and the keys hanging in the door. In my hallway, that was a definite no-no. Quietest night I ever had. On these and innumerable other occasions God watched over and protected me—even sometimes when I was not aware of any danger.

I cannot be afraid when God walks beside me. And though the world may think I'm crazy, I cannot curtail my activities because I have to go it humanly alone. Humanly or not, I *have* a Friend.

Having put my worries over life and limb behind me and continuing to see God's faithful intervention with my grades, I should have known trouble would eventually come my way. It's nice to remember that every dark night is followed by a promising morning. But no one likes to mention that our mornings also get followed by nights. And so it will be until that last great gettin'-up morning. Well, some unexpected surgeries in our family kind of flattened out the home reserves and what little I had saved was soon used up. Anticipating possible hard times, I figured that what the Lord could do once He could do a sec-

28

ond time, and so I struck out on the scholarship trail again. My budget was already more imagination than fact and, while I had reduced my food and·recreation expenditures to a minimum, there wasn't much I could do about the gasoline and rent requirements. I applied for a nursing scholarship, put it in the Lord's hands, and waited. In a matter of a couple weeks I was a jubilant recipient of a $600 nursing scholarship, which they said I could renew. Praise the Lord, and pass the corn bread! I unloosened my belt, treated myself to the zoo, and proceeded to turn my attention to other problems.

The time rolled around for me to go for another interview as a minor formality before they could renew my scholarship. The counselor told me not to think a thing about it. So I didn't. I planned out my financial strategy based on another $600, soon to be in my possession. I went to the interview. Same song, only a different verse this time. No money.

"What do you mean, no money? I thought you said it was a cinch."

The financial counselor just shook her head. I could see she was really sorry. "They said you sounded like you were going to be more missionary than nurse."

"But," I said, "I'll be putting in my 8 to 10 hours of nursing every day."

"Sorry," she said, "their decision is final."

I got up and walked numbly to my car. And then it all came out. I had stretched my budget just as far as it was going to go. I burst out into bitter tears and told the Lord I was about to starve to death. I really ranted and raved and said many things I'll regret all my life. It was so silly. But emotionally and financially that was just the final straw. I cried all the way home and kept crying for two days. I could see no way out of this one.

There was nothing to do but try to carry on. I had a bit

of reserve left from the last $600, and I apportioned it out to last as long as it possibly could with every economy move I'd ever heard of. I continued to try to earn a bit here and there. But I was required to spend so many hours actually nursing in the hospital by that time that there wasn't much time available. Funds continued to decrease as did food stocks and the day finally came when I started counting my money in terms of change instead of bills. My mother kept writing to ask if I needed money and sent some occasionally. One of her last remarks to me had been, "Jane, we'll sell the house if we need to, but we'll get you through." And they would have, you know! All their lives they have bent over backwards to give my sister and me all the things we needed. I thought to myself—I'll starve first!

I really can't express how sorry I feel for people who have never had to put God to the test, who had no one else to turn to but God. As long as I could scheme and stretch and make things do, God just let me carry on. Then when I could do no more, He stepped in and told my stormy life to "be still."

I can't tell you adequately how it all happened. First, there was Miss Stevenson, my former dorm mom at Pasadena College, who helped bridge the gap. I'd go over to see her, and she'd already have the table set for me, even though my visits were very sporadic. Not only would she feed me but invariably she would send me home with all the food my arms could carry. God prompted her, and she responded in His name. (What a reward He'll have for her someday!)

Then there were some friends from school who came over to see me. They had no knowledge of my financial straits other than the fact that all college students seem perpetually short of cash. They all came bearing food. Breakfast cereal for an afternoon snack? No, some of those things got thrown in because God directed. And when that was all gone, I got $10.00 in the mail from an aunt who had never sent me any money in my whole life that I could recall. Whatever should happen to me, I could see God didn't have starvation in mind.

I had come to the last three months of school and now there was no money for either the rent or gas. Since I had to have the car to get to the hospitals and school, I decided to let the apartment go and live in the car, perhaps in a campground, for those last three months. My parents had been living in Tennessee for quite a while now, and so no one would be the wiser. I anticipated some problems, but I wasn't going to quit three months short of a degree.

But I had calculated on everything but God. The phone rang and I casually answered it. It was the financial officer at school, whom I hadn't seen for several months. Considering there were about 20,000 students at Cal State who would be delighted to get a scholarship, I could hardly believe she recalled my existence. She said, "How would you like to have a Cal State scholarship?" I sat down. I said, "But I've only got three months left. Nobody gets a scholarship that near the end. Besides, what scholarship is this? . . . I didn't even know it existed. And I *know* I haven't applied for it." She said, "Nevertheless, it is yours if you want it . . . $300." *Heaven came down and glory filled my soul.*

I quickly went from my sitting position down onto my knees. I was so embarrassed I didn't know where to start. But amidst my sobs, I managed to get out the fact that I could now see how dumb I had been. God sure had supplied everything I needed, and, oh, how sorry I was for getting my eyes off Him. I got up from there a long way down the road from where I had been! I truly realized then that God's interest in His children is in no way a halfway thing. As I was committed to Him, He was committed to me.

So my counsel is: Don't worry about *things*—food,

drink, and clothes. For you already have life and a body —and they are far more important than what to eat and wear. Look at the birds! They don't worry about what to eat—they don't need to sow or reap or store up food—for your heavenly Father feeds them. And you are far more valuable to him than they are. . . . So don't be anxious about tomorrow. God will take care of your tomorrow too. Live one day at a time *(Matt. 6:25-26, 34 TLB)*.

3

Scotch Tape and Glue

One would think, seeing how the Lord was so determined to see me through those difficulties, that I would have been experiencing a real emotional and spiritual high. Well, the theory is good, but reality fell a bit short. The more I realized how much God was doing for me, the worse I felt. You can call that woman's logic if you like, but it's true, nevertheless. I was beginning the slow fall. I hardly realized what was happening, but I was falling in love with my God. And it seemed the more He did for me, the more I realized how little I was doing for Him. The more goodness I saw flowing from Him, the more wretchedness I saw within myself. I just seemed to fall so far short as a Christian.

About that time at school we began to utilize our psychology theory in some practical avenues. And I found myself exposed to the new and growing phenomena of sensitivity sessions. These sessions are so structured that groups of individuals come together for the express purpose of honest communication and evaluation of the members of the group. Individuals attempt to describe to other group members what their real impact is on the group. It gets back to what I mentioned earlier—about people saying one thing but meaning another. I was exposed to several such sessions in different classes all about the same time.

Initially I didn't feel too threatened. I mean, how could a nice Christian kid like me go wrong? I expected they might mention my use of sarcasm or my tendency occasionally to dominate a business session, but since I was aware of these things, I had cushioned my ego to take it. Unfortunately, it only took about five minutes to dispatch those things, and then they proceeded to make a bit more delving assessment of me. One of my teachers decided to come aboard and see if she couldn't straighten me out as well. As I look back on those sessions from this vantage point, I can't wish that I had never been in them. I truly did learn a lot of things I needed to know. But it is only the grace of God that ever brought me through them.

I had been in the habit of spending time in my car at lunchtime instead of eating with the other students in the lunchroom. For one thing it was cheaper to pack my lunch, and my thermoses were awkward to carry. But mostly I liked to spend the time reading my Bible since time for such things was at a premium. And I knew that in order to make any kind of a Christian impact on these kids, I was going to need a lot of fortifying. (Cal State's mascot isn't Diablo for nothing!)

I can only say I was one devastated Christian when to my amazement the turn of events brought my Christian witness and impact before the scrutiny of my classmates. I figured this was my best point. I had even taken a lower grade from one classs following a letter I had written to the school paper "in defense of God." Now they might not like what I was saying, but they couldn't argue that I was doing it. After all, I was going to be a missionary!

And then the axe fell. Again and again I heard how ineffective I was being. Why did I go to the car at lunch?

They never had a chance to talk to me about spiritual things for I was such an unapproachable goody-goody. And I said things all wrong. I was judgmental, I was a puritanist, I was close-minded, and I didn't really love people but only my cause. To top it off, "You'd make a rotten missionary. Why don't you change your major?"

To say that I took it all to heart and felt bad would be the understatement of the year. I went home and I started crying. I wept, and I wept, and I wept. Anything else they could have said to me I could have stood, but not that. I looked for comfort to the few in my immediate circle of friends, but they only seemed to verify all that had been said. I wanted to die. I hadn't called myself to be a missionary, God had. And I knew there was no other alternative open to me where God was concerned. So I had to be a missionary. But I couldn't be a missionary—and I was up against a blank wall.

The devil, seeing his golden opportunity, now proceeded to pelt me with the final blows. He carefully marched me down the lane of all my other inadequacies and, being quite a long road, I became very foot weary. I had really few friends in Los Angeles and no family within hundreds of miles. A guy I had dated a short time had dropped me like a hot potato. I supposed it was because he had seen the "real me." And what with the budget needing such close scrutiny, there wasn't too much chance of my going anywhere to get my mind off things. I'm sure the devil had a great laugh over it all.

Saved, sanctified, and miserable, I thought. How can this be? Somewhere along the line I had heard I was going to be perfect, but, I thought, I'm not perfect at all. In fact, I'm a mess. I tried to console myself by thinking about how the Lord had helped me subdue my fiery temper, but the devil pointed out 10 dozen other glaring troubles that stubbornly remained. I had no defense.

I was at the end of the rope again, but this time, instead of struggling to hang on, I wanted to let go. I just couldn't stand to have the Lord loving me so and my giving so little in return. Besides, I figured He had been standing there, pen and paper in hand, recording all those failures with an efficient nonemotional stroke of the wrist. Doomed in this life—doomed in the next.

Well, I thought, if a sanctified person is supposed to be perfect, I guess I must not be sanctified. And by the look of things I might as well throw the salvation overboard as well, for who would want to have a mess like me? I had cried for two solid days. Funny, I was studying crises intervention in school at the time, and I could analyze my descent into despair but not stop it. Always a fairly conscientious student, the day came when I awoke and said, "I'm not going to school today. I don't see any point in it."

My only alternative was becoming forcefully clear to me. I was convinced I was causing my Kind Benefactor more pain alive than I would dead. And my future as a missionary obviously held only disaster. Alone, beaten, and with no hope, I began to comtemplate the ways out of this world. It's amazing how unafraid I was. And I wasn't too worried about hell because I figured I was living in one anyway. I sat for a long time staring out at the rainy afternoon. I was a bit worried about what this would do to my family. I didn't want them hurt. But in my mind, I was somehow sure I was going to hurt them anyway. They would only believe the best about me and it was too much to live up to. What I needed was a friend, a real friend, someone who would like the real me. But there was no one. And so I sat alone with my thoughts.

The wonder of that day will stay with me as long as I live. I couldn't help myself. I was no longer looking for or seeking God. I don't believe my family or any other person I knew could have helped me either. There is no loneliness or misery like that of a failure, and I was labeled fair and square: unloving and unlovable.

As I contemplated my move, I saw my Bible lying there. I pulled it over. A fitting move for a funeral, I thought. I opened it randomly. And suddenly my Bible began to talk to me. These are some of the things it said:

> I saw myself so stupid and so ignorant; I must seem like an animal to you, O God. But even so, you love me! You are holding my right hand! You will keep on guiding me all my life with your wisdom and counsel; and afterwards receive me into the glories of heaven! Whom have I in heaven but you? And I desire no one on earth as much as you! My health fails; my spirits droop, yet God remains! He is the strength of my heart; he is mine forever! *(Ps. 73:22-26, TLB)*.

> For I know the plans I have for you, says the Lord. They are plans for good and not for evil, to give you a future and a hope. In those days when you pray, I will listen. You will find me when you seek me, if you look for me in earnest *(Jer. 29:11-13, TLB)*.

> "O people of Israel, you are saying: 'Our sins are heavy upon us; we pine away with guilt. How can we live?' Tell them: As I live, says the Lord God, I have no pleasure in the death of the wicked; *I desire that the wicked turn from his evil ways and live.* Turn, turn from your wickedness, for why will you die, O Israel?" *(Ezek. 33: 10-11, TLB)*.

> And so it happened just as the Scriptures say, that Abraham trusted God, and the Lord declared him good in God's sight, and he was even called "the friend of God" *(Jas. 2:23, TLB)*.

I had a suspicious feeling that those were more than the ancient words of my predecessors but God's words for me. I certainly felt like an animal. But could it be that God in full recognition of this was extending His hand to help me? That He didn't want me dead but wanted me as His friend? I put on some Christian records and read a bit longer. This was all very well, but I needed some explanation on some of these assorted problems I had, and there was no one there to explain to me.

I just sat there, against another dead end. Despair pushed barely an arm's length away, ready to pounce again. Then God, my busy God, took time out from the affairs of the universe to sit there on the floor with me and talk to me for hours and hours. Some of you, I know, will doubt that, but it stands true. I began to see and understand things I had never even thought about. I'll remember it as long as I live. It was as though God, looking in pity on the broken pieces, decided to put me together again. On hands and knees He began to Scotch-tape and glue, patch and mend. And while He did, He talked.

He explained that He wasn't out to see how quick He could gather condemning evidence against me. But He was there to help me. I knew I had heard that preached somewhere, but it had never quite gotten home before. To my chagrin, He admitted there were quite a lot of things in my personality that needed overhauling—more than I had even noticed thus far. But that didn't mean I should throw my salvation and my sanctification away as though they had no value. They were roadmarks of my progress, but they were positioned at the beginning of the road, not the end.

I said, "But I'm not perfect. I've got a lot of the same old hang-ups I've always had."

That was readily acknowledged. But He didn't leave it at that. "Jane," He seemed to say, "some people get deliverance from things instantly because that is what seems best to the Father. But in building a mature Christian, there is another factor to be considered, and that is personality. Personalties are developed by time, and it takes time to change them.

"When I point out something in your attitude or life that needs changing, you must begin immediately to chisel

38

away at it. And you must be aware that it may take a long while, and that, more than likely, when you're done, I may point out three other areas that need the same intensive care. But don't despair, just keep at it. Sanctification doesn't mean you are instantly a perfect being making no mistakes; that won't come until you see Me in the new world. Sanctification does mean that the Holy Spirit comes to live inside you and equip you to take on such an immense overhaul. It's Me living in you. Me as the Superintendent of Building and Remodeling in your life. But even more, Jane, it's Me extending the hand of friendship."

I just sat quietly, but my despair had had to move way back now. He continued, "Jane, when you talk to Me, you shouldn't just tell Me the things you think I want to hear. You did right when you thanked Me for the blue sky and for helping you on a test. It is good that you should ask for spiritual and physical help for those about you as well as yourself. But I am willing to be a lot more than Someone to whom you send your thanks and requests. You've had problems here; anyone can see that. Believe it or not, I want to share your frustrations, your failures, your disillusionment, your questions, your anger, and your tears."

I thought I could feel the tears of God in that room. And they were tears of sorrow and sadness and love *for me.* I thought to myself, Can it be that God would really be my Friend? I grew quiet. He was talking about my thoughts on suicide. He said that if I got too bad for Him to look at, He could bring me to my end. But as long as God wasn't ready to quit on me, why was I so determined to quit myself? As long as God saw there was hope for me, there *was* hope.

I felt like dancing around the room, but it isn't nice to interrupt, so I kept listening. "Jane, it is true you leave a lot to be desired, but I leave nothing to be desired. With Me helping you, you can do My bidding, even if the partnership is only 1 percent you and 99 percent Me. It can happen. But regardless of what comes, there is this to remember: You are not responsible for success in life, but only obedience. It doesn't matter how the world thinks you're doing, or if the world loves you. I love you."

Moments later, the tears had dried, despair had felt the door close behind it. I had found a Friend. And I thought the world could not contain me. I was rescued my third time down—fished out by a God who had been seeking me though my cries had long since been silenced. There is no way to express the way I felt for my Saviour at that time. I knew I would never again know the kind of despair I knew that day. And from that day to this, though often buffeted and confused, I have never known that kind of low again. If I ever think of death, it is only in reference to getting to my Father—not getting out of this world. While He needs me, I'll be here, just as He was when I needed Him.

The thing that amazed me most was that God was obviously prepared to love me in my state of disrepair. It wasn't, "Shape up and I'll love you." It was, "I love you just like you are. How about if I give you a helping hand with the repairs?" It was what I had always wanted. Someone with whom I could be perfectly honest—the real me—and be loved and accepted as just that.

Knowing that I had this kind of acceptance with my Lord, I began to practice the advice on honest communication. And it's one of the most wonderful things that has come about in my life. I find it's a lot easier and more beneficial to be honest with God, even with bad attitudes, than to spend the effort it requires to keep those attitudes in the back closet, pesky old problems that they are. It's even better to say something like, "Lord, You know how I feel. This just doesn't seem fair at all. Which obviously means my attitude and understanding both need a lot of Your help." It's better to have things out where God can work on them than to have them stashed beyond the reach of His healing touch. And though I've almost wondered at my own brazenness a few times, I can honestly say that whatever the problem or attitude I've presented God with, He has consistently met me with love. And if things needed to be changed, we changed them together. It's sure made life a lot easier for me not to have to expend all that time and effort talking myself into a better attitude. And God seems to be more effective with my bad attitudes than I am anyway.

There were a few fatalities along the way as I sought a clearer communication pattern between God and myself. God isn't hindered by the generation gap. He smiles, He laughs, He speaks my language. I've never found a limit to God's willingness to meet me where I live. The only limitations seem to be, so to speak, in my being home when he calls.

One false notion that had to go was oriented around the formalities I needed to employ in seeking God's presence. Somewhere or other I had heard some preacher say that he always liked to put on his suit coat when talking to God. Well, I had to admit this agreed with my Sunday worship concept of God. But if God was really going to be a part of my daily existence (and I couldn't conceive of a friend being anything else), then it didn't seem very practical for me to have to go and haul out my Sunday duds every time I wanted to talk to Him.

And what was more, I wasn't exactly sure where God would be pleased to meet me. I certainly hoped He would be agreeable to meet me some place besides kneeling at my bedside, since my bed got lifted back into its cubbyhole in the wall every morning. But where exactly could I and couldn't I meet God? I thought about Paul's admonition that we should pray without ceasing. And I figured that must mean anytime, anyplace, and in any condition. It's not that God doesn't deserve the respect of addressing Him in your Sunday best or in appropriate position in an appropriate place. He deserves it, all right. But He doesn't require it. I think He would rather you have the attitude of heart than the proper etiquette.

It was real fellowship we could have while I sat on the roof in my grubbies playing my guitar. And God would even let me talk to Him while I was soaking in the bathtub, or carrying out the garbage, or even watching TV. (I'm a television commentator—you know, the kind that likes to keep the rest of the audience up on what really has happened and on what no doubt will happen.)

Have you ever seen something really funny and turned around to share the laughter with someone and nobody was there? So I shared it with God. "Wow, God, wasn't that funny?" I just started talking to Him all the time about everything. There are so many everyday things to share, and besides I had years of backlog that needed to be aired. Such a patient listener He was.

But sometimes He had things to say as well. It took me a while to realize I needed to set some time aside each day for listening. I never leave those times without having learned something new. A person could get wise listening to God.

I think a lot of people don't really know what they're listening for when they listen to God. I know He speaks to different people in different ways. And what He has shown me might not be right for you. But you may be interested in what God has shown me. Now that I've said that, I'm not exactly sure I can really explain, but I'll give it a try.

Initially, I found I needed to set a special time for listening to God. First I would read my Bible, and then I would pray. Then I would attempt to get somewhat comfortable (at least where I wouldn't be restless) and ask Him to talk to me.

I have found fasting can be a real asset. I suppose then I thought I was making a trade with God—*my* piety for *His* answers. But I realize now that you don't corner God into doing something, because His actions are motivated by love. But fasting helped *me* to get serious about my pursuit of understanding from God. Somehow in letting go of food, I bring a lot of other things into perspective. And I am reminded that while I can do without a lot of things, I cannot do without God.

With one's mind in neutral, I find that God can introduce lines of thought. Not often, only rarely, does some great gem of knowledge fall from the sky. Too bad. More often I find my mind takes the avenue of inquiry and answer. You no doubt wonder what the quality or identity of the response is like. Is it a soft voice, a vision, a bolt of enlightenment? No, not really. I find the Lord has chosen to use the avenue of what we know as conscience. I know you're thinking, But that's awfully unreliable. That's what I thought, too, at first. But I find that if I'm really honest with myself I can tell if what passes through my thoughts is within the character of what I've known God to be and what His Son Christ and the Bible have portrayed Him to be. So you don't sit there and fight out all the thoughts that come to your mind. You use them.

I think the best example I can share with you occurred a few years later as I was driving my car across the Arizona desert. I was casually looking the landscape over when the Lord seemed to bring my attention to this one type of green plant. Now this was real desert and there wasn't anything else green anywhere to be seen. As I went on by, the Lord seemed to say via my conscience, "How, Jane do you suppose that plant manages to stay green out here in the middle of the desert where everything else has given up the effort and died, or at least turned brown?" I thought to myself, I don't know, I'm no botanist, and dismissed the whole subject.

But the Lord wasn't through. He said, "I won't accept that answer. Try again."

I couldn't figure out what the Lord was so interested in a green desert weed for, but as I had miles of straight road ahead, I attempted to bend my mind to the problem. "I don't know, I suppose it has something to do with the root system."

"Yes, go on . . ."

"Well, I suppose that its roots go down deep to get any moisture that might be down there . . . a hidden river or something. And I guess the roots maybe go out a long way to the sides too so that when it does rain, or dew, or whatever it does out here, it can get every last available drop in the vicinity. And that way, by taking advantage of every source available, it somehow manages to beat the heat."

I smiled to myself with satisfaction. Having the botany lesson behind me, I again turned my attention to the road. But class wasn't over yet. The Lord said, "How does a Christian stay green and alive when the whole world around him seems to be spiritually dead?" My curiosity was aroused and I said I didn't know but I'd sure like to. He said, "You tell Me."

So a bit blindly I started out trying to make the analogy. "Well, I guess you'd have to let your roots go down good and deep to a real Source of life. And I suspect that that means You, God. And I guess then that those surface roots must be out there to soak up every bit of blessing that comes by. Only you'd have to recognize a lot of different things as blessing. Sometimes there might be *showers of blessings* but sometimes there might just be *mercy-drops*. And I guess you'd have to take advantage of the enjoyment to be found in every little flower, and bird, and smile, and every little thing that came your way in lieu of a great flood

44

of spirituality among your comrades. I guess, Lord, you'd just have to be determined to use any, every, and all things to keep alive in the Lord."

And God said, "School's out."

I went along musing over that lesson for several hundred more miles. I don't know how often since then God has brought that object lesson to my mind to help me stay alive in a weary world. But that's what I mean by talking to God. As your heart is willing, He'll guide your steps as you seek Him.

4

Love Takes the Risk

It's interesting how God works in a person's life. It's the rare occasion when you can find a tree tall enough in your life to climb and see ahead exactly what it is God's planning to do with you. There usually seems to be mud on the windshield and you just have to move ahead by faith in the Navigator. On the occasions you think you do know how and why God is doing something, the years often prove that God was doing another thing altogether from what you had supposed at the time.

Such was the case for me when I arrived for a year of seminary in Kansas City. I thought I was there to learn about being a missionary, and I did learn quite a few things on missions while I was there. But really God had brought me to Kansas City for another, even more important, purpose. There was something I needed to learn, and it would certainly influence my success as a missionary. God has a lot of things He wants to teach us, and He'll go anywhere, and take you there as well, to help you to understand those things. Believe me, it's true, because I have had my training in a lot of farfetched places I never expected to see. But He always went with me—no correspondence courses with God.

It did appear to be a promising year that lay before

me. I was looking forward to my various seminary courses and anticipating my first year as a staff nurse as well. And, of course, this would be a last-ditch chance to look around for any new friendly people who might like to marry me. (I told myself I had stopped looking but deep down inside I knew better.) Those were the three areas in which I was hopefully looking. But the lessons which God had planned for me were on a different chalkboard entirely.

The main object lesson came walking in the door that first day and sat down on the far side of the room. I didn't even notice. But it didn't take very long for the Lord to get my attention refocused. My object lesson was the very best kind a person can have. She was fairly tall, a wee bit crazy, and prepared to love me on the spot. Now a girl friend may not seem like such a treasure to you, but we're considering me, not you, remember?

Now, as you may recall, I mentioned right at the beginning that I had spent an awful lot of my life saying hello and then good-bye to people. For those of you who have spent most of your lives in one or two places, it's very hard to understand what so much moving can do to a person's insides. For much of my life I had really enjoyed it, but enough is enough. I knew the arriving and departing had taken its toll on my life, but I had never come to grips with what that effect really was until that year. It was to be God's topic for the coming school year.

Not surprisingly, most of the students at seminary are married. But there were a dozen or so that had not yet tied the knot. We were a ready-made peer group. We all wanted God's will, we were all seminarians, and all single. It really was a fantastic year for me, due largely to those folks. Each and every one was lovable. But it took a while for me to figure out what I was going to do with them. Sound strange? Let me explain.

Relatively speaking at least, I think you could agree

with me that it is easy to say hello and quite hard to say good-bye. Everybody loves a homecoming, but farewells are always tearjerkers. New babies are celebrated, but funerals leave an emptiness. I had made a lot of good friends down through the years, people I had truly grown to love. But invariably, with time, I had had to say "So long." And every time I had said good-bye to one of those friends, I had left something with them. A piece of my heart followed each one of those friends.

I had hurt and hurt again until one day my heart said, It is enough. And I began to build the wall. I figured one more hurt and there wasn't going to be any heart left. It doesn't mean I turned a cold shoulder on everyone. But I could only let a friendship go so far. This never proved difficult because I was usually moving again before anything more was needed. And, although no one particularly seems to believe me when I say it, meeting people, or audiences, or guys, scares me silly. I don't know the proper way of doing things even today, college degree or not. And I'm the world's best at unintentionally getting my foot into my mouth. I just say dumb things sometimes—most times. All those factors combined to make new friends a bit of a perplexity to me. I could smile and say hello; I could invite them over for a party; but I had my limits—and God was out to destroy them.

God had a tool. Her name was Barbara. She didn't lecture me or advise me, counsel, or instruct. She just loved me. And I noticed she was loving quite a lot of other people as well. She really cared about the men at the rescue mission and the children in her Sunday school class. She even cared about their mothers! She wasn't manufacturing concern and love for the folks she was staying with. She really cared. And all the singles were her special burden, and from the greatest to the least she had time for them.

Walking perfection? Not hardly. She got tired, and frustrated, and upset just like me. And she got hurt too. But there was something different there. No scar tissue seemed to form on her heart. She was perpetually tender. I stopped and took a good look at the state of my love. It was a pitiful sight. Scarred and shriveled up, it was a far cry from what God talked about and Barb demonstrated.

I began to talk to God about it. "Lord, I know I'm supposed to love God, country, and family. And I know you ask Christians to love their friends and their enemies alike. And I have always tried to do that. But somehow I'm missing out. What more is there?" I felt like the wealthy young ruler and half expected to hear Him say, "Go and sell what you have and follow Me." I should have known better, especially since I didn't have much of anything to sell.

But instead, He had me go over the list again. Starting at the top. "Jane, do you love Me?" "You know I do, Lord." "Jane, do you *really* love Me?" "Lord, You know I do. Why, I'm Your buddy, Your good friend." "Jane, are you? Are you really My friend?" I wanted to cry, "Lord, You know my heart; You know I'm Your friend and that I love You." "Then feed My sheep." The darkness was beginning to become light.

It's not sufficient to go into a little corner and love God while He loves you. It just doesn't work that way. God loves you, then you love other people, and that is how God knows you love Him.

My being a missionary must not be a job; it must be an expression of love. God loving me, then me loving other people. When not on the mission field, it was me loving the folks around me, the people in my country, my church, my family. Love, like a fragrance, goes everywhere and seeks out all who are there. And love, like a fragrance, is not selective on whom it falls. Let's face it, the tall, dark, and handsome ones are easy to love, as are the witty, the charming, and the intelligent. Even your enemies—maybe because of the pure challenge of it—can be not so difficult to love. But it's the wallflowers, and the grumpy little ladies, and the undisciplined, impudent little kids that cause the problems. It's the person who seems to need your time for some triviality when there are monumental events that need your attention. *Love* is a very big word.

Not only was the scope of love a lot larger than I had suspected. But as Solomon said, "Many waters cannot quench the flame of love, neither can the floods drown it." (Song of Sol. 8:7, TLB). True love doesn't develop scar tissue. True love just keeps taking it, and taking it, and taking it. That was hard for me to accept. I don't like getting hurt. No one does. But love doesn't let hurt stand in the way. I would suppose that none of us can really comprehend how Christ's love was abused. He just went from one man to the next, loving him. And in return they mocked Him, laughed at Him, spit on Him, and in the end crucified Him. But He never stopped loving. And for that matter, man has never stopped abusing. Like I said, love just keeps taking it, and taking it.

I knew within myself that I had done many a thing to hurt my Lord, but all I ever found at His feet was steadfast love. There's no insurance policy issued with love. Love means being "at risk." Love is being susceptible. The object of your love may wallop you over the head. Or, if you're trying to love publicans and sinners, the "righteous world" may just label you as one of them. Gossip may fly.

And if you're a single girl trying to carry on a nice, platonic relationship with a guy who just needs a pal, I send my condolences. Even your best friends, who should know better, will rib you with comments on your new "boyfriend" despite your greatest efforts to demonstrate to the world that the "friend" part is all that's involved. You might as well save your breath, your friends are *going* to tease you. But in the final analysis love doesn't really care what people think; love is intent upon its purpose.

"Lord," I said, "that's really beautiful. But tell me one thing: How can I love other people? I want someone to love me!" It sounded like a fair question to me. And as the Lord always takes my sincere questions seriously, He answered me.

"Jane, *you* love other people, and *I'll* love *you*. It's kind of like I'm asking you to be My funnel—a channel for My love. I'll pour love into you, and you let it flow out to others. The faster you let it out, the faster I'll fill you up, because I won't ever let you be without love. But if you put your finger on the bottom of the funnel so that the love can't get out, the better to preserve it for yourself, it will just evaporate. Then you will be without love. Jane, will you be My funnel?"

When He asks you like that, what can you say? "Yes, Lord, a thousand times over, yes! But God, You'll have to remove the scar tissue and set about to teach me this new way." It was agreed, and even to this very day He is still widening my vision. I have a long way to go yet, but for a worthy goal one can afford to be patient.

You know, the greatest tool the Church has is love. Not the "Hello, how are you?" kind, but the "How are you *really*?" kind. The Church can't compete with the world for entertainment, lavish facilities, or fancy clothes. But it doesn't need to. Because what the world wants—every last single soul out there—is love. And we could love with a love like the world has never known. Love people as they are, where they are—presalvation, presanctification, plain, old, ornery people. We could love them. But I wonder if we are doing it.

51

5

Where, Lord, Where?

They were before me at last! Those missionary application forms. A lot more pages than I had figured on. I reckoned I had waited enough years; it was time to make the big move. Of course, once those applications were in, things would be pretty final. I laid them back on the desk. More than anything else in my life, I wanted God's will. I wanted to do what He wanted me to do. But I just wasn't sure what that was. I suppose you know the feeling. I've thought on countless occasions how nice it would be if we received gold-engraved letters from heaven. *Memo from the desk of God.* With such a concrete directive in my hand I'd be willing to do anything, literally anything. But without it, I sometimes get cold feet.

I think it has something to do with my trying to get a better look at the road map instead of just patiently waiting for the simple "Left at the next corner." I suppose it's because I want to get things "just right." The only trouble is, what I think is just right isn't always what God has in mind. For instance, I figure "just right" and "success" have got to lie on the same road. However, Daniel did things just right and ended up in the lion's den, Jeremiah at the bottom of a well, and David nearly got harpooned to

52

the wall dutifully playing dinner music for Saul. But who's going to deny these men were successes in God's eye? See, it's your vantage point that counts. The way God sees things may just not coincide with the way you're seeing things. And in the final analysis, God, not Merriam-Webster, defines success.

The Lord pointed this out to me quite clearly one day. I was fretting about how I was going to fit in on the mission field. I never really did fit my own concept of what a missionary really is. Missionaries, amazingly enough, are just plain people. But I was pretty sure their plainness was several notches above mine.

Besides, I seemed to fall under the category of just a little bit wild and woolly. I mean, how many girls do you know who like to ride motorcycles and fly planes? And how many missionaries do you know who like to listen to Dylan and fly kites? Also, I knew that new missionaries are supposed to kind of conform and keep their silence for the first few years while they learn the ropes. It's a good rule, road tested for worthiness. I was, nevertheless, not too sure I could "toe the line" that long. One thing I sure didn't want to do was muff up any of the Lord's work.

So I hesitated, and have hesitated on more occasions than one. I find reading my Bible really is a help to me when I'm walking the valley of indecision. If you expect the Lord to use what is in your mind to communicate with you, it seems only fair that you should provide Him with some ammunition. There was a day when I didn't really enjoy my Bible very much. I read it because that was the thing a Christian does, but I wasn't really getting that much out of it. I think it began with Pastor Earl Lee in Pasadena. The new translations helped too. But somewhere along the line my Bible came alive. I reasoned—correctly, I hoped—that if God would allow me such freedom in talking to Him, I might also use that freedom in reading His Word.

With a wealth of painting, television portrayals, and history books telling me so much about those days gone by, there was no reason to keep the Bible characters two-dimensional. I knew what the men from Galilee looked like, for I'd seen lots of them in the pictures at Sunday school. And I certainly knew what Roman centurions looked like, for I had seen them following Caesar around on the television Tuesday night. And I knew what the country side looked like, because Coalinga is often compared to the Bethlehem area.

Now, since I love a bit of drama, I decided to try taking a few of those characters off their pages. Setting the stage before me in my mind, I decided to see what they would do. I watched Peter tell the Lord how he would die before he would deny Him, and I was impressed with the assurance with which he said it. Then I saw him go out and do the very thing he had said he would not. That's rough, you know. I felt sorry for him. Then when he had broken into tears and gone out, realizing his blunder, I followed him. I wasn't sure that theologically I was on sound ground. But God didn't seem to be calling me back.

When I found Peter, I saw and heard some amazing things. Peter was the very picture of despair. Sitting in a puddle of his own tears, he seemed to have no hope. He wasn't calling out to God; he was talking about ending it all. I thought, This guy looks suspiciously like I did that day in Los Angeles. About that time, God started talking to Peter. He told him how much He loved him and that he was forgiven. And then He got down and glued and taped Peter back together. After acknowledging Peter's faults, He said, "We'll work on them together. Don't end it all, Peter. I have a job for you to do."

I thought to myself, How about that! I never supposed there was anyone else who had gone down that road. I flipped a few pages and looked again. Old Jeremiah and I

54

had loads in common, and Moses and I felt about the same way concerning being God's spokesman. Since then, I've not had the heart to corral my Bible characters back into two-dimensional still-lifes. Regardless of which translation I'm reading, it's always a "living Bible."

God has multiplied His use of the Bible in speaking to me. I can't read my Bible enough. It's become nearly my favorite pastime. Sometimes while I'm praying, I read some scriptures as I go. And while I love my commentaries, it's pretty exciting what you can get straight from God. So it is that when I come to a crossroad in life, I take out my Bible to see what the fellows before me did.

I have noticed a very interesting thing: None of God's men ever got lost. Lots of times they weren't too sure what the Lord wanted them to do or which direction they were to go. But it always worked out for them. Further, I realized that if you really want God's will for your life, and not your own choices, God will see to it that you get on the right path. So there is no real reason for God's children to quake and quiver every time they come upon a new decision in their lives.

This is going to be a bit confusing, but see if you can follow. When you turn your will over to God, you don't go around will-less the rest of your days. God replaces your will with His will. You want to see your brothers and sisters meet the Lord. You want to see love and righteousness abroad in the land. Now, I ask you, what ordinary man on the street is going to tell you that what he wants in life is love and righteousness abroad in the land? I know, you're smiling. That's because men's wills aren't like that. The reason a Christian can honestly say that he wants to see love and righteousness throughout the land is because it's not original with him. He is only reflecting God's will.

Did you follow that? If you did, we can go one step farther. There is a great deal to be done in this world. Right?

Well, who do you think is going to do it if you and I don't? It's all very well to say that God is going to do it. But, friend, whose hands and feet do you suppose He is depending on using to get the job done?

Now, I'm not encouraging impatience in finding out what God wants you to do with your life, for there is no doubt that God uses the delayed answer in teaching us many things. "Patience develops strength of character in us and helps us trust God more each time we use it until finally our hope and faith are strong and steady" (Rom. 5:4, TLB). But I would like to encourage the aging gang on the starting blocks to go ahead and shove off.

Don't be afraid of doing what you just *think* might be right. Your mind will tell you if it's completely out of the context of what God has in mind for you. God isn't going to let you go way off in left field. God *loves* you. God has a plan mapped out and, like any good plan, it has some timing factors involved. God needs minutemen who are willing to respond without a 12-month warning of "signs in the sky."

One day as I walked to work, I approached a man on the sidewalk. God said, "Tell this man I love him." I thought, Really, God, that's a bit much, don't You think? I mean, he is going to think I'm some kind of a nut or something. By this time I had passed the man, crossed the street, and was only wondering at the craziness of the things my head suggested. But as I started to walk on, the Lord just dumped one huge load of His sorrow and disapproval on me, and I knew I had really blown the situation.

Not wanting to spend the rest of the day in misery, I wheeled around and yelled at the top of my lungs at the man who was by this time standing on the opposite corner, "Say, did you know that God loves you? He really does!" Now, if I was worried he was going to think I was crazy before, I didn't have any doubts now. Sure, I obeyed. But how much better if I had done it on first prompting, and then perhaps had a chance to really talk to the man.

I don't know what was happening in that man's life, but God was counting on me for intervention, and my hesitancy very likely blew the whole thing. I'm not suggesting it is easy to decide on something, especially something that may well change the direction of your life. I'm just saying, Don't wait so long that the tide carries you out in its ebb.

Something else along that same line. Those of you who have snow-skied will know just what I mean. But for those of you who value your limbs at a higher price, I'll elaborate. When learning to make a turn in the snow on skis, you have to be moving fairly fast down the mountainside—the faster the better. Now this is a strange paradox, because nobody wants to start down the mountainside until he knows how to turn. You figure if something looms in front of you, you want to be able to avoid collision. But skis are so long and unwieldy in snow that it takes the reduced friction from traveling at some speed to make the skis manageable enough for such maneuvers.

We aren't always manageable enough in God's hands for Him to get us turned in a new direction until we've started moving. But I have found that once I'm moving, I find the assurance of His direction as He makes His will known to me.

6

The School of Hard Knocks

It takes time to really establish a friendship. There's no denying that sometimes when two folks meet, they just click as though they were made for each other. But even then their fellowship isn't half of what it's going to be a few years hence when they've shared some experiences together. For instance, my parents periodically get together with some of their friends from years gone by and not infrequently the subject of the depression comes up.

Now, I've studied a bit about the depression in school and have seen a few films on the subject; therefore, I like to make my contribution to the discussions. But it doesn't seem like I ever get more than about three words out when I'm met with the rejoinder, "You just don't understand, Jane. You weren't there. You don't really know what it was like." And I have to admit that my firsthand recollections of the occasion are rather limited, probably more like nonexistent.

But you know, my parents and their friends can spend hours talking over those old days. And while they describe them in the most forlorn terms, I think it's one of their greater delights today, judged by the frequency of conversation. Not because of its toughness then, but because of the way it enhances their friendship today. They have known hard times together, and sharing the memories of those hard times today adds a depth of understanding to their relationship. Quickie acquaintances, however well matched, can never take the place of these. I have found that my relationship with God works on much the same basis. I've never particularly liked the hard times in life, but I'll have to admit they have brought me closer to the Lord.

I think it's important that the Christians in this world not only recognize this factor, but begin sharing it with others. I have a strong feeling that a lot of young Christians are really troubled by what they suppose are their own isolated difficulties in serving the Lord. If all you ever hear during the midweek testimony service is, "Thank God, every day I spend with the Lord is a delight," or, "I've served the Lord for 43 years and never once have I wanted to turn back," you're bound to be disillusioned. It can be pretty discouraging when that day comes along which, far from being "a delightful day in the Lord," is more like one pain from beginning to the end. The first thing the young Christian wonders is whether he has come by a counterfeit experience somehow. You hope that somehow during his devotions he'll come upon Job declaring, "Though he slay me, yet will I trust him."

Why doesn't anybody ever testify, "Today the well went dry, the electric company turned off our lights, little Jenny broke her arm, and I got fired. But, praise the Lord, I know there'll be a better day someday!"? I heard one man do it in Scotland and, oh, how it blessed my heart!

Let's face it, life as a Christian is not always a bowl of cherries. Yes, there are superwonderful days, but my experience is that there are some very, very rough ones as well. The devil is a sly old character. And if there is a vulnerable spot in your armor, you can be sure he will find it

59

and make the best use of it. Not every day as a Christian is a joy, but each day is worthwhile and can be satisfying. It's a chance to make history with God working in, and around, and through you to bring that bright new day. All this so that some day you can look back and say, "God, it's great what we've come through. Now I know what Joshua said is really so: 'You know very well that God's promises to you have all come true' (Josh. 23:14, TLB)."

Now a hard knock is a different thing to each individual. It may come in the literal form of a dented fender, a busted leg, or a broken heart. But more often than not it's a bit more subtle. Often you don't even know what it is until you are in the midst of it. And it may come in the most unsuspecting circumstances. Maybe it will be a program you've nurtured at church that turns out to be a royal fiasco. Maybe it will be your well-intentioned hard efforts getting slung back into your lap. Maybe it will be expecting a raise and receiving a demotion. I'm sure you've each encountered a few hard knocks along the way. I came upon one just about two years ago that really threw me for a loop.

Seeing as how I'm told Swaziland has the highest birthrate in the world, my more experienced mission comrades felt I really ought to take up midwifery before joining them in Swaziland. So I found my first appointment as a missionary was to Scotland! Well, that was all right because I love atmosphere, and Scotland is loaded with all kinds of neat old places that positively shout King Arthur, not to mention a lot of wonderful folks of the present era.

I arrived expecting there would be some minor problems, such as reversed traffic patterns and the perplexing challenge of keeping peas on the back of one's fork while transporting them from plate to mouth. But that was about the extent of my anticipation of difficulties. I had no idea I was about to get *knocked,* par excellence.

To my dismay, it soon became evident that my nursing registration was not going to be accepted until I put in three months' duty in one of their hospitals. During those three months I would have to work as a nursing auxiliary, or aide as they are known in America. Oww! That hurt. Worse yet, they decided to put me in a surgical ward. Now I had just left a job of some responsibility in a surgical intensive-care unit in America. And while it doesn't take too long to get the feel of power and authority, it is another matter altogether to have to lay it down again.

The nursing service in Great Britain is structured quite a bit more formally than in America. Interpreted, this means, everyone knows his place and stays in it. There was no place for a nursing auxiliary to attempt to flaunt her B.S., R.N., and P.H.N. I had a clear-cut job, and I was to learn to do it efficiently. I know I would never be able to express adequately what it feels like for a nurse to see things that really need to be done, like a dressing change or an addition of an I.V. bottle (especially when it's something she has been doing for several years) and yet have no power or freedom to do it. Frustration! And as though that weren't bad enough, having no power in my own chosen specialty seemed downright silly.

Let me tell you the rest. I've never minded the manual parts of nursing, whether it be bed making, bedpans, or breakfast in bed. And I naturally figured with a nursing degree I wasn't going to have any trouble with those areas of endeavor.

Bro-ther! Having an ocean between us makes a lot more difference than just an accent. In Scotland, bed making has become a fine art. They don't do it anything at all like we do in the States. There are all kinds of fancy little innovations that require a fast hand and a keen eye. And they don't just make beds once a day. There are regular bed-making rounds, made at least four times a day. If a person reads the paper and gets a little newsprint on the bedspread, you change it. And if the sheet is a little wrinkled before the doctor is due to come around, you change it. And if the matron is coming, you better believe I can throw clean pillowcases on pillows faster than a flitter. And it's not a bedspread, it's a counterpane. It's not an injection, it's a jag. And it's not nurse; it's "Hey, Yank" or "Miss America."

I really didn't mind the patients kidding me. I think some of them understood my troubles better than the other nurses and tried to kid me out of them. But I really was confused. I couldn't be a nurse. And I could see right off, it was going to take some time to be a decent British aide, even though I was working six and seven days a week (trying to get my three months' experience done in two and one-half). I probably should have, but quite honestly I didn't "live rejoicing *every* day." I got a few feeble thank-yous out, but usually for the remembrances of "days gone by." Mostly, I hung on to the Lord for dear life . . . waiting for the silver lining.

The day came when I could finally pack by bags and leave to pursue my original purpose—midwifery school. The Lord asked me, "Well, Jane, what did you learn?"

"What do You mean, what did I learn? I can make a fancier bed than most Americans have ever seen. And I can strain porridge like it's going out of style. And I can . . ."

"Jane, you know that's not what I mean."

I thought for a while. "Lord, I see that there is no shame at being on the bottom of the totem pole. A lot of my fellow workers, and the gang in the kitchen, and the ones who dump the garbage are a lot better folks than some of the ones who hold the desk. At least I can see it's individuals that count and not their job titles. I think the next time I'm in charge of a ward I'll have a lot more understanding for my subordinates than I ever had before. I see that it is You who sets up rulers and kingdoms, and who can take them down again."

It was a hard lesson to learn, but it has been a worthwhile one for me. And occasionally when times are a little rough, I think, "God, it was great how You brought me through those first months in Scotland. Remember how I was so cold, with the snow on the ground, and You warmed me up? And how I felt the day I was caught clanking the bedpan when Dr. Clark came around?" You know, because we went through those things together, it has deepened my relationship with God. It was hard, but God's reliability held me together.

When I got to Swaziland, there was another hard knock of sorts. Ever hear of culture shock? Yes? Well, I was all prepared for it. I wasn't going to stare at any odd manner of dress, or complain about the food, or faint if I saw an unusually large bug. And I did admirably, I must say, with those things. But I was surprised to find my culture shock coming from an entirely different direction.

I was prepared for missionary life, and missionary life suited me fine. I loved it, in fact. Everything that is a bit "rough and ready" is right down my alley. But I didn't realize that that is only one portion of missionary life. I, who hardly ever can remember if the spoon or knife goes next to the plate, was suddenly invited to attend exquisite meal after meal as a form of greeting when I arrived. Somehow I never expected my lack of Amy Vanderbilt background would present much of a problem on the mission field.

Thanks to the good-heartedness of the folks at home and the ingenuity of our missionaries, the mission field does not fall short on the social graces. While not extravagant, there is definitely the chance for good fellowship over a well-laid table. This is great, except I'm the picnic-table, TV-tray, kitchen-counter type. And for what I was encountering, I was unprepared. But the Lord is good, gracious, and very understanding. And He giveth more grace.

I don't think it's very realistic to think Christians will *always* be found smiling. People who always smile can't be doing too much thinking. There is a lot of sad stuff in the world. Spiritually as well as physically, life presents its problems. But one thing is true of the Christian life. Hope springs eternal. After all, God's on our side! Sooner or later that smile ought to creep back. Frowning can be habit-forming. If you've been short of a smile too long, best talk to God about it. And there's no real point in waiting till things look more promising. Joy doesn't really know the confines of a situation. Joy is this: God loves me here, now, and a whole lot.

7

What's a Spinster Anyhow?

There are some things you don't discuss in mixed company. Not guys and gals mixed, but married and unmarried mixed. And one of those things is "old maids." Now I know from my youth that it isn't at all uncommon for housewives to discuss: "Who can we find for Sally?" Or, "Don't you suppose old Matilda gets lonely down there on that farm? They say she's got lots of money and doesn't want to share it." Or, "I feel sorry for old Marge. Maybe if she had a face-lifting . . ."

I'm sure you know the kind of conversation I mean. Bachelors are discussed in the same way, although I'm not sure to the same extent. And, speaking from the ranks of the singles myself, I can assure you that we periodically hash the problem over among ourselves. Probably not as often as you might suppose because the subject can be slightly painful. It has the ring of defeat, although I often think unfairly so. There is the added fact that it may also call up an assortment of sad memories of days gone by. It just doesn't represent much in the way of a pleasant evening's topic. At least not for the subjects involved.

Although several authors have already applied themselves to the subject, I feel there is more that needs to be said. You're going to laugh when I tell you this, but I almost omitted the subject for fear I'd be married by the time you read this. I figured you might think that would invalidate what I'm saying. But since this is not a very likely turn of events, what I am about to say is a valid, if subjective, statement on the situation. Besides, I figure if writing a chapter on being single is going to get me married, I should have written one years ago!

It's a very interesting situation to see the years go by as a single. First your high school chums get married, then your college colleagues, and then the few left among the ones with whom you work. First you're a bridesmaid, then a maid of honor, and then maybe back to a bridesmaid. And you begin to realize your girl friends look to see where you are before they toss their bouquets. And your friends casually mention that the fellow you used to date now has twin sons. And when you go to baby-sit, some adorable little girl says, "Are you a mommy?" But it's amazing how the human spirit withstands all these abuses. After all, you tell yourself, don't all those Hollywood starlets say they wouldn't think of marrying 'til they are at least 26 or 27? They say they haven't lived 'til then.

I remember thinking while I was in high school, I just bet I'll never get married. My freshman and sophomore years in college I didn't think too much about it; I wasn't even too sure I was ready. My junior and senior years, I decided I was as ready as I would ever be, and set a sharp lookout. The first couple of years after college, I decided I would just do without. I'd show them; I can make it on my own. The next year, I zapped the other direction and thought, "Oh no, I'll never survive . . . I just cannot stand it . . . I refuse to go down this way!" And then, finally, this year I've found peace. Interested to know why?

It wouldn't be fair to the "other" characters in my story to tell you, fellow by fellow, what I've learned. The facts are I learned more of it from God than I did from the fellows anyway. And my real intention isn't to tell you how to live life alone. I suppose you just basically do what comes naturally. I'm more inclined to think I address myself to you worried families, friends, and neighbors. I guess I would just like to explain our phenomenon to you.

Most of us are single either because we never found the right guy or because he never found us, and less frequently because the timing was wrong or the Lord shook His head no. I think the kindest thing with old maids would be simply not to assume that nobody wanted us. For one thing, most girls can rustle up a tale of some pursuer back there *somewhere*. And even for the girl who in all honesty can make no such claim, there is the fact of exposure. I mean you can only marry the right guy if the right guy is around. And let me tell you, some places are preciously short on their supply of "right guys."

Actually I stand condemned in that statement. Guilty. You recall I mentioned I had dabbled in the baby business? Well, we were certainly an excited bunch of student midwives who approached our first few days in the labor ward. We could hardly wait to go rushing back to our rooms that night with our tallies. "Okay, how many babies did you deliver today? How many boys, how many girls?" First night: three girls; second night: three girls; third night: two girls. I began to worry. I was afraid to ask my expectant mother what she wanted for fear she'd say a boy and I would feel I had to go get another midwife. "Sorry, lady, I deliver girls only."

Sharon Jones, another missionary from Indiana, had joined me in Scotland by this time, and between the two of us we delivered about 20 babies before we ever got a boy. We were feeling terrible! I felt like all I was doing was delivering old maids. After all, what chance were they going to have in 1990 if I hadn't provided any males? Thankfully, we evened things up a bit before we left.

But seriously, there really can be a dearth of the right fellows. Invariably you married folks always know just where we can find the right guy. But really, I can't honestly say that I find matchmaking very helpful; it can be terribly painful. You just can't imagine how embarrassing it is when an unsuspecting fellow and girl show up at a friend's house to find they have been paired off. If it's a couple that can laugh about it, they'll survive. But some people are just a bit too reserved to be able to acknowledge the obvious situation with a laugh and so determine just to endure it. I think it is fair to say that most of us singles would rather you didn't try to find us a man. But, if you're determined, at least talk it over with us first.

I also mentioned the variables of timing and God's approval. It is very frustrating to have a fellow show up just as you are about to leave the scene. You immediately consider, Should I stay a bit longer? But, unless you have had some "real" encouragement, it seems like a rather forward and foolish move. And besides, depending on what you were headed for, you may not have the alternative of waiting. It is a very sad thing, in some ways, that girls don't have greater freedom in initiating interaction with their fellows. I suppose some of us would amaze the world if such a thing were allowed. But there is a certain cultural taboo that forbids such things. Whether women's lib will ever really change this remains to be seen.

Usually it's not too difficult to decide if you have God's approval. But there are times . . . Sometimes an honest scrutiny of God's Word makes it pretty obvious. Don't be unequally yoked. Don't be a man's second wife unless the first one is dead or was adulterous. Don't just look at the outside; God evaluates the man on the inside. Most of us know what the Bible says and agree it's very clear . . . until you're in love. The obvious cure-all for these problems is to avoid the situations. And that sounds awfully good in theory, but it's not always that simple in reality. I can tell you right now that if you are single and you play with fire, you are going to get burned.

Testimony time. He was such a nice fellow, just wandering amidst the paintings on the mall. And he had good taste too; that was obvious because he liked my paintings. Obviously of a degree of affluence; new, in a strange town. Any girl in her right mind wouldn't turn down a friendly dinner date with this new arrival in the fair city. After all, just one date. What could it hurt?

It could hurt plenty! It was about the fourth date thereafter that I realized the guy was getting serious and my own heart of stone was melting fast. I considered my alternatives. You get out now while the getting's good . . . or you hang in there . . . and maybe he'll become a Christian. That's always a favorite line to fall back on. But, as I honestly peruse the list of the girls and guys I know who married non-Christians, I have to be honest and admit that a lot more lost out themselves than ever won their guys or gals over. Isn't that so?

I decided to apply the brakes after a friendly invitation to church got shelved. He never was antichurch; on the contrary, he made it a real area of intellectual pursuit . . . but he wasn't going to let it near his heart. I'm really thankful to the Lord for trying to ease the pain. The last evening I saw the guy, the Lord helped me hear how loud he rattled as a result of the emptiness inside him. But, even with that knowledge, I admit it hurt quite a long time.

Still, that's a fairly straightforward situation. Now we get to the tricky stuff. How about when you are both Christians and you are still not sure? You may think that is uncommon, but I assure you it is not. All the variables may seem right, but a Christian still wants to be sure of her "Father's blessing." He must be more than just an "acceptable" guy; he must be the "right" guy. In fact (especially if you've been a bit of a long-term old maid), is there supposed to be a guy at all?

It is amazing how often I have to explain to the folk of the world that missionaries do not *have* to be old maids. Hubby must meet with the approval of the Department of World Missions if you are going to serve as a couple, but marriage is not forever barred from you. Still, you don't find very many who get to the mission field and then marry. We thank Him for everyone that has and is, but such ones are, in fact, in the minority. Want to know a secret? We here on the field have noticed that second and third furloughs are the most promising. My colleagues will probably shoot me for saying that. Ah, well.

The problem yet remains: How to know God's will on this matter. You may think, Why not just ask God like you do on everything else? Well, that's a good question and deserves answering. I'm not sure my reasoning is very sound, but I am sure of what it is. We somehow feel that where the heart is so deeply concerned we just might unintentionally be guilty of slanting the results. A bit fearful that the old conscience might just say, "Sure, go ahead and marry him," all on its own and without the Father's approval. I'm not sure that since we trust God to communicate to us on all our other issues that it is reasonable to feel so unsafe at this time. But it happens nevertheless.

Then you may say, Why not search the Scriptures? Well, I've tried that too. There are two basic themes: one place tells you it's all right to marry and the next says it's really better to stay single. They don't contradict each other; they just afford two good alternatives. The problem is they are the two you already knew existed. You can choose one to back up your decision, but in the back of your mind you know the alternative is there. It just doesn't have that taste of finality the heart craves.

So, what are my ideas? Well, it is going to sound a bit flimsy, but you just have to wait on the Lord. Believe me, nobody can tell you whether you should get married or not. And nobody should try to. It's among you three. Get up your courage and pray about it together. If you're too shy to mention marriage, then just tell the Lord that you are becoming awfully good friends and is that all right with Him? Read your Bible, pray, and then listen. It may not come in clarion tones like you'd prefer, but scrupulous honesty will bring you to a conclusion.

As I said earlier, God loves you and He isn't going to let you walk past your probable mate without a hint. Nor is He likely to allow you to get hooked up with the wrong person without some bad vibrations. Trust God and do what seems right. And, yes or no, make a decision. It is terribly unfair on a thing like this to keep your counterpart in the dark for eons. It hurts.

Well, if you decided to get married, I'm really glad for you. I am—honestly. But if you have decided to remain a "one" instead of becoming a "two," then I've a bit more to say. Sometimes it is going to hurt. I mean that. It's going to be painful. Tears occasionally, discomfort sometimes, awkwardness frequently. That's life. I think that if you can't bring yourself to sharing your tears, it is good at least to talk with someone about the matter. And you know best who that might be. Everybody knows it is sometimes lonely to be single, so why waste your efforts denying it? There are better things to do with your energy.

Now as to the discomfort. Do you know when it is most uncomfortable to be single? It is when you are surrounded by one or more blissfully married couples. That's why singles tend to bunch together. When you see some guy come over and tell his wife he loves her, you can't help but think,

Ahhh, isn't that sweet. Followed immediately by a sense of loss on your part.

I think it is, nevertheless, important—vital even—that singles find a home, especially one with children where they can feel a part. If you're married and have a family, it is a great kindness to open that home to a single. Not for dinner or a party, but for helping the kids make cookies in the kitchen, or just watching television on a Thursday evening. Being single doesn't mean you don't need family. But if you are going to offer yourself as a family, you have to offer the major ingredient—love. If your marriage is just "too good to be true," don't be surprised if your single can take only an hour or two of it at a shot. She isn't covetous of what you have in the sense that she wishes she had it and you had a wart on your nose. She just wishes she had it too.

Sometimes you can sneak by for days on end without a single stab at your marital state. But sooner or later it catches up. It was in a church in Scotland that I first heard a wedding announcement given like this: "We are pleased to announce the marriage of John Doe to Mary Brown, spinster of our church." I sat there horrified. I looked around, but only we Americans seemed to have our mouths hanging open. It's a common term there, without the particular flavor it has in the States. But I cringed anyway. I wish that word had never been invented. It leaves such a taste in the mouth. So Eleanor Rigbyish. I'll have you know we old spinsters have life left in us yet.

In fact, I might as well speak to that. Just because we aren't married doesn't mean we are senile or juvenile. And very few of us will lay claim to being helpless . . . more likely a bit too independent. I've heard it said that we rely too heavily on borrowed husbands to do repairs and heavy work. I deny it, I deny it, I deny it! There may be a few guilty parties, but the average gathering of singles will usually reveal enough plumbing, electrical, and building experience combined with the brawn of these elusive butterflies to make a mighty thing to behold.

What is more, you can expect us to show up most any place. And if you're single, and don't, you're crazy. Don't let the lack of an escort rob you of the pleasures of life. Just smile and carry on. That brings to mind the ski slopes again. On a busy day, double occupants are preferred on all the ski-lift chairs. So if you are by yourself, you stand and yell, "Single," until someone joins you for the ride up. It's a very commonly heard cry as skiers are always getting separated. One day a kind, middle-aged man looked pityingly at me as I yelled, "Single," and said, "Don't worry about it, honey; you'll find your man someday."

Well, the world will always have jokers like that. And quite honestly, some days you'll want to laugh with them and other days maybe cry. But the great vacillation of spirit over this one area of life does eventually begin to smooth out. At least it did for me. Not just because I became accustomed to the idea or found myself a little bit farther removed from prospects, but because I finally got God's message. I was so sure that I needed my man—that I needed to get married. But not so.

In the final analysis, all I really need is God. Yes, I need Someone to get me up in the morning and help me keep my budget. I need Someone to validate my worth in the world. I need Someone to love me, and I need Someone to love. And God has met my every need.

I can hear it in the back of your minds now, but you think I won't say it. Well, here goes. How about the physical needs of a young single woman? Maybe you think a single person doesn't have the same physical desires and needs as you married folk do. Well, let me tell you, we do. We are not some kind of subnormal freaks. We are made just like you are. So what about those physical desires?

What does God do with those? Well, I'll admit that I don't exactly know. But when I feel those desires begin to clamor for attention and I know that there is no morally legitimate way I can satisfy them, I ask the Lord's help, and He brings me through to the other side. God doesn't ask you to handle *any* of your problems alone. He *can* and *will* meet your *every* need.

I have about decided *that* was a very important lesson for me to learn. I believe it will always help me to keep things in perspective. If I marry, fine (let's continue with the honesty); it would be super great. If I don't, ah well. But whether I do or not, I will always know God is first in my life. With no disrespect to a potential husband, I can take you or leave you. But God I've got to have. And isn't that what Jesus meant when He said: "If you love your father and mother more than you love me, you are not worthy of being mine; or if you love your son or daughter more than me, you are not worthy of being mine" (Matt. 10:37, TLB)? A husband can rate very high, number two even, but number one must always belong to God.

8

Think Big

As a Christian concerned about your fellowman, do you ever look around and feel kind of, well, kind of overwhelmed? There are so many people in so many places with so many problems. And believe me, if I keep delivering babies at the rate I have the last couple of months, there aren't going to be any fewer to worry about tomorrow. Besides the pure number, people are so scattered about all over the place. I suppose that seems self-evident. But I had never traveled much outside the United States until the last couple of years. And I declare, we don't have any corner on the market in numbers.

I always realized there were a lot of people around this world, but you have to squish through an open-air market in Tunisia, or fight the traffic of Marseille, or move into a huge city in South Africa you hardly knew existed to get the real feeling of people, people, people, *everywhere*. And every last one of them with problems.

Isn't that a bundle of cheer? Well, I've not said anything that isn't true. As long as I'm laying out the gloomy details, I might as well finish all at once. We, as the Church of Jesus Christ in all our various manifestations, are not keeping up, let alone excelling. And that means there are a lot of people carrying heavy loads right straight into the depths of hell. I know that's not a pleasant thought, but you can't dodge the fact.

If we could really see the world the way God sees it, I wonder how we would feel. We lead sheltered lives. Ignorance is bliss, and all that. We know only a lot of our friends, neighbors, and countrymen are bound for destruction. We've never really felt any pangs for the Hungarian trailer-park attendants, the Maltese horse and buggy drivers, or the Rhodesian train engineers. Out of sight, out of mind. But God sees all those folks and many more. And God cares. He really cares. Nothing casual about the way God feels about people, *all* people.

Most of you have been in love some time or other. How would you feel if you could see destruction heading toward that object of your affection? What if you couldn't reach them, but there was someone standing close by who could avert the calamity? You'd start hollering your lungs out so that person might intervene.

Need I say it? God is crying out to us. Each of us. No, not the person on your right, nor the one to your left. They have a job, too. But there are some people whom only *you* will ever reach. I'm serious. Everyone casts his shadow. There are some people who require your influence, however much you may wish to think otherwise. You may be wishing I'd change my subject, and I half wish I could too, because I feel as uncomfortable in this seat as you do. I would just love to pass the buck. "Lord, I know the very person You need to do the job. She is sitting right over there two pews down and to the left. Why not go ask her (him)?" Sorry, Charlie, God needs *you*.

I can hear it all now. "That's very fine for you to say, Miss Brewington. You that God has showered with talents, and know-how, and ability. But I'm just a poor, retiring personality without a single talent to my name. God couldn't possibly need me." Rubbish to both the fore and aft part of that sentence.

I'm going to enjoy these next few paragraphs as a chance to vent some "righteous indignation." I will admit, but only very provisionally, that some people do seem to have more talents than others, but most people could do a lot more than they are doing with talents they either haven't recognized or just haven't bothered to use. My mother has often said, in reference to being asked to do some task at church, "I'll try anything once. And if I'm not any good, I guess they won't ask me anymore."

It really makes me sad to see preachers practically on their knees begging people to take some responsibility at church or in a program. The pastor shouldn't have to beg; he should be able to retain a bit of dignity. How would you like to spend half your free time trying to recruit people to help you present programs in *their* church? I suppose most ministers would need to be seated while you told them you were going to volunteer your services. They might fall over in a faint.

Besides, how do you know you can't do it 'til you try? So what if you tried once before and you muffed it? Practice makes perfect. I decided a long time ago that God gives every man a certain amount of skill and a great, colossal bunch of potential. He gave us our senses and an ability to think along with the desire to do more than just stay out of the fire.

You learn a trade so that you can feed and clothe your body. Why not learn a "trade" to glorify God? My philosophy is to learn every possible thing you can. Interested in painting? Tackle it. Is the gas man relighting the hot-water tank? Pay attention so if need be you can do it yourself sometime. Friends with Bible commentaries? Borrow one. Don't just sit there and vegetate.

You say you are just too busy. Working a double shift,

just had quadruplets, and you have 492 quarts of string beans to can. Believe me, I'm really impressed, but that's no excuse. Interesting, isn't it, how you can always count on the busy person at church to handle just one more thing? I'm not saying with a schedule like that that you should enroll for 16 units in your nearby night school. But if you read just one chapter of one worthwhile book a day or just practiced singing in the shower, at least you would be trying something.

Very often the Lord decides to use some pretty strange talents—ones you didn't ever figure on being displayed before the public or semipublic eye. It may take the very best cherry pie in town to make the old codger down the street accept an invitation to church. Or knowing how and where to turn the water off when your neighbor's pipes are broken may provide that long-awaited time to talk about "living water." You just can't tell in what disguise opportunity may present itself. Therefore you must be prepared for anything. You say that means "jack-of-all-trades, master of none." Maybe. But God doesn't need your expertise; He needs your willingness. God uses the simple to confound the wise. A skilled craftsman can do amazing feats with the very simplest of instruments.

It's really true that a lot of missionaries are not all that skilled. It's just that missionaries are not allowed to say no. It's one of the rules of the job. A missionary tackles anything. Sometimes we bungle it too. But remember, success is God's province. Ours is but to be ready, willing, and obedient.

One day when the Lord was talking to me about being a missionary, I prayed, "But, Lord, missionaries go out to save the world. I can't save the world. I can't save the city I'm living in. As a matter of fact, I'm not sure I could tackle this block. How about if I just worry about the corner here on Birch and Seventh Street?" To my chagrin, the

Lord agreed I couldn't save the world, city, or block. He also included my corner as beyond my capacity! In fact, He said I couldn't save anything. Not even myself! People don't save people. God saves people. If I have any part to play at all, it's more like that of a stagehand. You've heard Shakespeare's line, that "all the world's a stage," haven't you? Well, God is the Actor on the stage. He is the One who is doing things. But He needs willing people to "set the stage."

You've heard them called planters and harvesters. But who is it that makes the grain grow? It's a hard thing to understand that God needs us. After all, He's got all that power; surely He could take care of things alone. Now, if people were "tuned in" to God, He *could* help them. But most people are not tuned in. A lot of people don't even have enough basic information to know where to dial to get tuned in. Or, just as bad, they have so many misconceptions and so much wrong information they aren't sure they *want* to tune in. Why should they even think God in heaven cares, if nobody here on earth does? God loves us; therefore, we love other people.

Have I got a recruit? Fantastic. Now I know what your first question will be. What is the strategy? Obviously, with such a big job to do, it won't do to just rush out there pell-mell with no organization. I wondered myself what the strategy was. I sat there with a studious look and prepared to hear the worst: Step *A*, Step *B*, Step *C* (refer to Step *A*, Part 3), Step *D* . . . But it's not like that at all. There is a plan, and it is quite short, sweet, and to the point. But, it is very hard to remember. It's this: LOVE. I know, it looks too simple. But the facts are, it is most effective. Everybody likes it. Who doesn't love to be loved?

But, although love is much appreciated by everyone, it is very often used as a last resort. I honestly believe it is easier to spend an hour passing out tracts (and that certainly has its difficulties) than to spend equal time really loving someone who is, well, unlovable. Loving means risk, and sharing painful problems, and giving something of yourself to another person who may not give anything in return. All the other things we do in and for our church are important. But without love, what is it worth?

Now that you know the plan, the project lies before you. Not your corner, nor the block, or city. There it lies —the world. You thought we had finished with such gargantuan projects, didn't you? Not hardly. Can God be satisfied to see our "left over" go to hell? I don't believe my Bible allows for that. Christ tells about leaving the 99 to hunt for the 1 lost sheep. Today it's more like leaving the 1 to look for the 99 lost sheep. The needs are great. Too great for us. But not too great for God. God *can* save the world. That is just about the right size job for God. And, since it's possible, can we aim for less?

No, I'm not blind (nearsighted, yes, but not blind). I can see there are some rather great difficulties in approaching such a huge (to put it mildly) task. The most obvious one is where to start. Love in the home is as good a place as any, and then in your church, neighborhood, town, country. Love finds a way. I must agree that a person's influence does have limitations. The chances of your average Alabama housewife influencing the baker on the main street in Moscow are rather limited. But that doesn't mean she's all washed up or is not useful in the Kingdom.

It says in the Directions Book (otherwise known as your Bible) you are to pray to the Lord of harvest to send out more reapers. That means you are supposed to ask God to send somebody where you (mind you, where *you*) can't go. If it is within your range, then you may as well assume you're God's man of the hour. But for what lies beyond your grasp, there are other people who could be recruited. God is asking us to care enough about the people we aren't

80

reaching, and maybe don't even know about, to ask for some help.

I must admit, it is not very easy to understand how what we ask and do influences God. Maybe if He were a little god of stone or wood that had to be carried about from room to room, that might be. But He is the God who made the universe, the proton, and the daisy. What possible influence can we have? Are you a big brother or sister? If not, I'm sure you at least know of some. Have you noticed how parents rely upon the older kids to watch out for the younger ones? They don't love one better than another, but they realize with growing up comes responsibility. It is right that older children should care for the younger ones. God is our Father. We are His children. With our growing understanding and knowledge of God comes responsibility, and the responsibility is named Mark, Sarah, and Terry (better known as the world).

Somehow or other we have made asking things of God a very tricky matter indeed. First you have to make sure it's an "appropriate" thing you are asking for. Then you have to ask "just right." And then, of course, you have to be careful you aren't interpreted as demanding it, because you aren't at all sure it is going to be in God's will. And you had better not look too soon, because you just don't know when God would want to do it. No wonder a lot of people never get beyond: "Now I lay me down to sleep, I pray the Lord my soul to keep."

When Christ said we were to be like little children, I believe He meant in a most unsophisticated way we were supposed to read God's Word and believe what it says without having to read between the lines. Now, using that hypothesis, what does this mean?

> Ask, and you will be given what you ask for. Seek, and you will find. Knock, and the door will be opened. For everyone who asks, receives. Anyone who seeks, finds. If

only you will knock, the door will open. If a child asks his father for a loaf of bread, will he be given a stone instead? If he asks for fish, will he be given a poisonous snake? Of course not! And if you hardhearted, sinful men know how to give good gifts to your children, won't your Father in heaven even more certainly give good gifts to those who ask him for them? *(Matt. 7:7-11, TLB)*.

Now that doesn't seem so complicated to me. That seems pretty straightforward, in fact. Remember when Christ thanked God for making things understandable to simple men that even wise men couldn't comprehend? Our gospel is meant to be simple—straightforward, to the point, and uncomplicated. God didn't mean for us to lose out on possible blessings because we didn't understand a complex formula. When God says, "Ask and you'll be given," He simply means ask and you'll be given. When He says, "Seek and you'll find," He simply means seek and you'll find. And if you knock, then you'd better stand back unless you want to get hit in the noggin with a door.

You think He is giving us too much responsibility? God is our Father. He loves and trusts His children. Remember, we aren't will-less. God gave us His will. And He wants us to use it in redeeming our brothers and sisters. He delights in giving us good things. And He delights in working with our brothers and sisters.

So start asking. Don't get hung up on what and how to ask. When I go to ask my dad for something, I don't get an ulcer over how I'm going to make the petition. I just say, "Hey, Dad, how about fixing my car for me?" I know he loves me and doesn't expect me to submit four copies of a work requisition form. God isn't trying to trip you up. God is anxious to see something done. Go to a loving Father and make your heartfelt requests known. He desires your presence before Him. And, as long as you're going to ask, ask big. Why not? Christ said: "You can ask him for *anything,* using my name, and I will do it, for this will bring praise to the Father because of what I, the Son, will do for you. Yes, ask *anything,* using my name, and I will do it!" (John 14: 13-14, TLB).

Now, "anything" doesn't mean just something small; it means *anything.* And since God has all the resources and power of the universe at His fingertips and our needs are so great, why are we so obsessed with the small stuff? We serve a great God, so why do we spend so much time shrinking and cowering, trying to get up our courage to ask for a little shower of blessing? He has tidal waves of them waiting while the world sits in the dust.

See any blind getting their sight lately? How about the dead being raised to life? And no less dramatic, how about souls turning to God? We could be seeing those things, you know. "In solemn truth I tell you, anyone believing in me shall do the same miracles I have done, and even greater ones, because I am going to be with the Father" (John 14:12, TLB).

I'm not casting stones. Honest, I'm not. But deep in my bones I'm feeling more each day that I've been spending my time in a little puddle of God's power when there is a whole ocean right beside me. It sounds so positive when Christ says: "Listen to me. You can pray for *anything,* and *if you believe, you have it;* it's yours!" (Mark 11:24, TLB).

I have been praying for quite some time now for a revival—a *big* revival. And just a few months ago, God told me it was on its way. It seemed so clear to me that I felt it was cheating to say I was now believing. Who wouldn't believe a personal announcement from God saying it was coming? I believe God is desperate to have the world brought to know Him. Could He have given His Son in any less of a state? I can't list for you all the things that are in or out of the will of God. But this I do know: It is God's will

83

that souls be saved. Go ahead and pray, I assure you it is God's will.

Have you ever noticed how much easier it is to ask God for something *sometime* than to ask for something in particular *now*? It takes a great deal of faith to ask God to turn this week's Sunday services upside down. What is the phrase? "But I don't know if it's God's will," or perhaps, "We aren't ready." Right! So, when you phrase it, put the shoe on the right foot. God IS ready! And God will do it when WE'RE ready! If you get serious about revival this Sunday, God will get serious too.

Having trouble believing? I know it can be hard. But look, has God ever failed you? No! Well, He hasn't failed any of the other millions of Christians either over the last few thousand years. What kind of a recommendation do you want? Something more personal? Well, I'm no tower of strength myself, but of late I've started getting serious about asking. And, you know, He's been serious about answering. Yes, "ask *anything,* using my name, and I will do it!"

To the fields, reapers!

9.

What a Way to Go!

In effecting a project as large as the one we have just talked about, there are two factors to be considered, one a variable and the other not. God is not the variable. He is the same yesterday, and today, and forever. He was reliable for Abraham, He is reliable for you, and He'll be reliable for your greatgrandchildren. *If* you ask God to do something, He will do it. It's a big *if*. And it points in the direction of the variable. "If only *you* will ask." I wonder how often the oiled wheels of God's progress stop at our front door. Has God already done a lot for you? Are you feeling a bit gluttonous from the blessings you have received?—"Keep on asking and you will keep on getting" (Luke 11:9, TLB).

I don't think God means for you to worry about it. When He really starts blessing, well, "let the good times roll." Do you know I have heard people say they asked the Lord to stop blessing them because they knew if He blessed them any more it would kill them? So what? What a way to go! I can't think of any way I'd like to exit this world that would be better. "Here lies Jane Brewington—blessed to death." I like it, I like it!

I have another thought along that same line. Do you ever feel as though you are already so pressed that to try and do one more thing would wipe you out? Believe me, I know the feeling. I have wished that Solomon would have said a little less in Proverbs about all the painful consequences of

"A little extra sleep,
A little more slumber,
A little folding of the hands to rest" (Prov. 24:33, TLB).

It's not like I really want 12 hours every night, but if I were always sure of 7 or 8 it would be nice. But, really, there just isn't much time to sleep during a crisis. That was demonstrated by the doctors and nurses in World War II. Following bombing raids they worked in the operating rooms straight through the long nights. It was either that or have no patients in the morning.

Well, you may not like to face it, but we are living in a day-by-day crisis, only it's souls we may well not have in the morning. Christ said not to worry about things that could only kill the body; it was the soul that really mattered! Are you tired? Rest in heaven. You are God's variable. How much can you take? As I comtemplate it, I think I could be just about as happy with this: "Here lies Jane Brewington—worked herself to death for the kingdom of God." That doesn't taste half bad either. I think it must be better to put in a few really worthwhile years for God than a whole safe score of them twiddling your thumbs. We've got supervisors enough; we need some laborers.

Don't worry that the odds are against you. While I was in Scotland doing those three months as an aide, I often thought about what I might try to do for the Lord while I was in midwifery school. And since it was only three to four months until I would be there, I thought I'd plan ahead. But when I was reading my Bible, the Lord brought me to a standstill in the Gospel of John: "Say not ye, There are yet four months, and then cometh harvest? behold, I say

86

unto you, Lift up your eyes, and look on the fields; for they are white already to harvest" (John 4:35).

I said, "Lord, You can't be saying what I think You're saying. I don't know anybody here. And I can't even completely understand their accents yet. And there is just no way, no way!" It's amazing how unimpressed the Lord can be with my soliloquy at times. I didn't have the foggiest notion of what I could do. So I began to pray and fast. It's as good a way as any to kill time when you want to retard progress. I continued this for a month. (Now, I certainly don't mean to tell you to stop praying and fasting any more than I mean for you to stop breathing.) Since I had an inkling of what God wanted at about one week, what was I doing during those other three?

Finally I saw that it was now or never. So I ventured forth from the prayer closet. God had suggested I put on a musical production to bring the scattered Christians together and to bring that large hospital's attention to God. I had approximately two and one-half months before I was to leave. Do you have any idea how long it takes to put together a musical program, even if you have everything available to you? I was working so many hours in the hospital, there was hardly any time to work on the musical except late evening and into the nights.

I'll admit to you I figured I was on a wild goose chase, but to keep my name clear with the Lord I thought I'd just give it a wee go. Mind you, I had just arrived in Scotland, and I knew *nobody* before I came. Well, there is no point in going through all the details, but the Lord provided (out of the clear blue sky, as far as I was concerned):

One 16-voice choir
One auditorium (with props)
A number of great songs I had never even heard of
A choir director
Two guitars

A set of drums
An electric organ
A spotlight or two
And, last but not least, an audience
You could have bowled me over with a mothball.

Well, shut my mouth! God is not the variable. The variables I've already named—YOU and I.

You may think, "But there is ability, girl; there is ability." No excuses, folks. I flunked Spanish. And because of that I have spent many an hour dreading my Zulu language study here in Africa. The Lord said, "Nonsense! You have to learn this, Jane. How are you going to tell people I love them if you can't tell people I love them?" It seemed a valid point. Besides, remember—where God guides, God provides. I've just taken another Zulu test and passed. It doesn't matter about your ability, not when God is on your side.

I guess what I'm really trying to say is to get out there and do your level best, and God will do the rest. But don't wait for the proper time or the right conditions. This is the day which the Lord hath made!

But none of your other friends are doing anything very radical? *That's the trouble!* Don't worry about what the other fellow is, or is not, doing. When God calls you before Him on that great day, He isn't going to discuss how your brother-in-law or Mrs. What's-her-face got their jobs done or their quotas filled. He is going to be talking about what *you knew* to do and what you *actually did.* Are you squirming in your seat? I was feeling a bit restless myself.

Now concerning God's resources—the ones He has given to you for safekeeping. Don't be stingy with what God has given you, or, like your love, it might just evaporate. I heard a pastor in Scotland share this analogy: Giving your resources away is like the man shoveling coal from his coal bin who, far from running out, seemed always to have an increasing supply. When queried, he replied, "I shovel out the front door and God shovels in the back door, but God has twice as big a shovel."

Amen, brother. There is an absolute rule of the universe: You cannot outgive God. When I gave up my nursing job in the United States, I thought that with upcoming reduction in salary I could quite justly say, "Good-bye, good times; hello, hard times." But honestly, I can tell you it just hasn't happened that way. I wouldn't suggest you therefore just forget your missions offerings, because (1) every time you deposit something in the plate for the mission field in God's name, He deposits a great reward for you in heaven; and (2) though you are indeed generous with what you give, the real miracle is in the way God is multiplying your best efforts to provide more than we could have hoped for.

Whether your generosity is pointed in the direction of missions, or someone's school tuition, or groceries for your pastor, be prepared for what God has promised: "I will open up the windows of heaven for you and pour out a blessing so great you won't have room enough to take it in! Try it! Let me prove it to you!" (Mal. 3:10, TLB).

That guy Solomon. Now there was a smart fellow! They say he was one of the richest men that ever lived. No Wall Street advisors, no bank consultants—just read his own proverbs, I guess: "It is possible to give away and become richer! It is also possible to hold on too tightly and lose everything. Yes, the liberal man shall be rich! By watering others, he waters himself" (Prov. 11:24-25, TLB).

10

Are You Sure
About That, Lord?

Now it seems a bit pointless for me to spend any time on how to get through a good day. Most any lame-brain can properly handle days full of sunshine, paydays, and vacation days, given no other complicating factors. My only thoughts on that rosy state of affairs is—be aware of your good days. Savor the smell of the grass and the sounds of laughter. Someday those memories may be more precious than gold to you; so collect a wealth of them.

Now as for those other kinds of days, well . . . One thing is for sure, there is no getting around gray days. So that leaves only one alternative. You've got to go through them. Well, maybe I shouldn't say there is only *one* alternative, for there are others, but they don't seem to cut the mustard. You can go the route of denial and try sleeping 23 of the 24 hours. Or you can join the Jonah club and try running away. If you can find some unsuspecting chump, you could try "passing the buck." But funny thing how a person gets to the place where he has just slept all he can sleep, run all he can run, and passed that buck as often as he can pass it. Demoralizing, isn't it? But ever so true.

So you crank up the old record player for "I never felt more like singing the blues," grab the Kleenex box, your Bible, and your favorite chair. Then with a big, if quavering, breath you look it in the face.

Trouble wears a lot of different disguises. I've seen many more of them than I would care to recount. And I realize I'm not unique. One thing about trouble, it ain't pleasant! Have you ever been so far down you felt like you were looking up at the bottom? And another thing about trouble: When it rains, it pours. Oh, my, "Stop the world, I want to get off."

Now there are two basic categories under which we can distribute your average range of problems: those you've caused yourself and those caused for you. The first bunch has a double cutting edge: the problem itself and the "you should have known better" agony. The latter group, though single-bladed, can nevertheless cut you to the quick pretty effectively, and sometimes they are impossible to rectify, being completely beyond your own grasp.

Now, for once, I have so many super illustrations I could choose from in my own life, I'm kind of at a loss as to which ones to use. No real reason to go back umpteen years, I guess. How about a month or two back? Black Monday is bad enough; but if it is topped off with gruesome Tuesday, villainous Wednesday, unmerciful Thursday, and unrelenting Friday, you begin to feel yourself a bit persecuted. Not everyone can claim their own "national disaster area." As I prepare to list some of the troubles, I realize they aren't going to look quite so bad to you as they did to me; secondhand troubles just don't have the same bite that your own new ones have. But at least it will establish a setting for us to talk about.

I had taken a Zulu exam just before that week and was not expecting exactly real super results from it. I mean, the book says "Zulu," but it's all Greek to me. And the test had been a bear. Now it is bad enough to do poorly on an exam, but it is twice as bad when you know folks are sacrificing at home to put you through language school, not to mention the fact that a missionary who doesn't speak her adopted language is a bit of a useless phenomenon. Sure, I could still provide nursing care, but there are a lot of fine Swazi nurses who can do that. I want to tell people about Jesus.

Well, that was the first thing. Then my brand-new, shiny motorcycle got racked up by someone I didn't even know had borrowed it. So there were going to be sizable repair bills and a precious lot of walking facing me in the immediate future. Than I had this wonderful (perhaps half-baked, but wonderful) idea about a witnessing project here in the local shopping center. My previous efforts with a Bible study had not seen the results I had hoped for, but I was sure this would be different. I excitedly went to church to tell my friends, and *powie!* They riddled it with holes so fast it nearly took my breath away. I walked home with one more punctured balloon.

A few other similar episodes occurred, and by the end of the week I was quite the worse for wear. Then the devil, seeing his chance, tripped me up on something I hadn't had trouble with for several months and I hit bottom with a thud.

I was beat. They say you either have to be an anvil or a hammer in this world. I was definitely feeling like the anvil—pounded to death. I suppose most of us are the same. You take it, and take it, and take it until one day you decide you can't take it anymore. First it was only a trickle, then a stream, and finally a torrent of words and tears that started escaping into the room. Who was I addressing? Who would listen to such a barrage of hostile nonsense but the Lord? He's amazing—He really is!

I would love to have sounded like the offended saint, but my conscience couldn't swallow the idea. I berated myself. I berated my plight. I berated all the people and factors that had gotten me into such straits. And, even though indirectly, I was sort of berating God as well.

I then did something I haven't done since I first set out on my own—I asked God if I could just go home. "Lord —please, Lord—I want to go home. I'm making one royal mess of things here. And what I'm managing not to mess up, others are messing up for me. It isn't fair!" I was on pretty shifty sands, so I started grabbing for some scripture or something to back me up as the "injured party." So it was with due delight that I grabbed this one and half flung it at the Lord: "And we know that all things work together for good to them that love God, to them who are the called according to his purpose" (Rom. 8:28).

Aha! I guess I really thought I had the Lord cornered. Well, live and learn. I wouldn't suggest you try that tactic with the Lord. It took Him about two shakes to turn that scripture around and tie me in a knot with it. Once He had me so contained, and a little silence finally prevailed, He asked me this: "Jane, where has that ever not proven true?" I thought—my golden opportunity. "Well, Lord, there was that time when . . . No, forget that. But then there was last year when . . . Nah, forget that too."

I thought, Why am I on the defensive? I've got a perfectly good case right here. I said, "Lord, this time it's not going to work. I know I have a lot of faults, but I *do* love You, and I am called according to Your purpose. But nothing good is going to come from this racked-up Honda." I would never have admitted it then, but as I look back, it sounds almost like a dare, doesn't it?

I'm sure the Lord realized it was pointless trying to dent such a determined stance, so He just told me to hit the sack and get some rest. Maybe He was hoping I would get up on the mellower side of the bed. But not me. I figured this state of affairs deserved at least a couple of days of moodiness. So I pouted through the day till midafternoon when I had to go to the university to find out how I did on the Zulu exam. I dragged myself over, thinking the mission station language board was likely to send me packing when they heard about this. I eyed the score sheet, starting at the bottom.

Honestly, I can say in my whole life I've never been more amazed at any test results. I not only passed, but I passed jolly well. And yet the last week of class I had hardly been able to answer a single question put to me. But not believing God had sent me to Africa to "spin my wheels," I had kept repeating: "Lord, (gulp) I'm expecting a miracle." And I had then spent much time in staring at my textbook. I didn't exactly know what I was staring at, but I kept thinking, If I donate the time, maybe God will donate the Zulu.

As I started home, I knew that I personally had been part of something exciting. Despite my tantrums, my doubts, my inabilities, God had given me my miracle. I didn't want to cry, I wanted to kick myself. But that being anatomically difficult, I settled for crying and dressing myself up and down a few dozen times. "Jane Brewington, I can't stand you! Here God is always bending over backwards to help you, and encourage you, and all you do is complain and gripe." Only I was much more detailed and vehement in saying it.

I had to admit the Lord had done very well by me on that test. And I soon was able to see other means of witnessing opening up, probably more effective than my earlier plans. But my motorcycle continued to thwart my efforts at seeing any good come from its dents. "Really, Lord, honest, I just can't see it. I mean, I could grasp at straws and say no doubt all these miles of walking now are making me robust and healthy (not to mention affording me blisters). But surely that's not what You had in mind when old Apostle Paul said things would work out for good." Of course the thing about people is that we always want to see all the reasons for our situations *now*. Demanding bunch, aren't we?

In time, of course, I saw the good God had intended from the situation. The gal that had been responsible for the damage to the bike turned out to be a young woman who seems to have had a rough time in life. I got a letter from her that made it sound like she ate nails for breakfast, splinters for lunch, and thorns for dinner. Real friendly sort, you know. I only had to read the letter once to know exactly what God was wanting. So now I write fairly regularly to her and I'm loving her for Jesus. It's really not hard, either.

She doesn't write back, so I don't exactly know where I'm getting. But I do know that God wants me to persist and that He knew this was the only way (sacrificing the Honda, that is) I would ever have known how badly this girl needed loving. Besides, God owns the cattle on a thousand hills, and He can provide me with functioning cycles without any great ado. (I haven't exactly decided how He manages that, but He does.) And motorcycles aren't nearly as important as people. Sometimes the whole story takes a long time to come together, but all things *do* work together for good, and for *His* purposes.

Well, that was fine. That cleared the deck of all problems currently imposed on me by others. This was fine, except that, with the debris cleared away, I was left looking like an eyesore. "Lord, how is it that I have such good intentions, and keep ending up in such hot water?" I started getting a reply to that so fast I got the impression the Lord had been waiting a long time for me to ask that question.

He had a lot to say about it too. It took Him several days, in fact, to get it all said.

Vaguely, it centered around my long-range planning. "Lord, in these next few weeks and months keep me from these temptations which so easily beset me; in fact, forever would be quite nice." The Lord pointed out that that kind of prayer was not very realistic. Temptations are a part of life, and the devil is going to make sure that plenty of them fall across your path. Nothing lazy about the devil, but slyness galore.

It seems that when you've just come through some battle and God has replanted your feet on solid ground following your wallow in the mud, that that is when you are really ready to fight another battle. "Come on, Devil, just bring it on. I'll show ya! Come on, let's have a battle—I'm ready for you." Of course, nothing ever happens then. Life goes along like milk and honey. The devil's no dope. He patiently waits till the morning comes that you wake up and think, You know, things are going so well, I don't think I'll buckle on quite so much armor this morning. And so you skip your devotions or cut them so short they are anemic. And you swagger out to meet the world.

If you had really tremendous hearing, you probably would notice the snare drum setting the atmosphere as you walk to your fate. Now you aren't suspecting it. Now you aren't prepared. *Now* the Devil lays you low. Then, as you lay there staring in the mud again, you think, Where did I go wrong?

The Lord had me review the course of events on several of my own strolls off the gangplank. And every time it correlated. When I thought I was really stable, I was about three inches from taking the dive. Sounds an awful lot like "pride goeth before a fall," doesn't it? I know that since the Lord had diagnosed the problem so well, He no doubt had some specific remedies in hand, so I settled down to hear them.

He reminded me of the words I had heard from an alcoholic who had been off the bottle for a couple of years. He had said that *every* morning when he wakes up, he asks God to help him not to drink that day. Not that week, or that year, but just that day. And I realized as I thought of that, that I had no business getting farther from the Lord, or the reality of my weakness to temptations than "Lord, help me to live for You *today*." It isn't that God couldn't help you a year from now. He can, remember. But *you* forget that you need help. So now when I wake up, I think about the things that so often trip me up, and I pray, "Lord, today, deliver me from such and such a temptation that so easily besets me." And He does.

But that isn't the only thing about my long-range planning that bothered Him. He said, "Jane, you're kind of inflexible in My hands." "Me? Why, I'm a veritable ball of mushiness; what are You talking about?" But I realized He was right.

Maybe because I've moved so much, or gone to school so long, I'm not sure, but I do tend to like to have my itinerary planned well ahead of time. It doesn't have to be a minute-by-minute itinerary; hour-by-hour is quite sufficient. After all, we mustn't waste any of the Lord's precious time. There is too much to do for that. The Lord seemed to appreciate that. But He kind of took me back when He said, "But Jane, don't you think we ought to have a closer relationship than one where I have to submit a projected plan three weeks in advance in order to assure your cooperation?" Hmmm, I thought, that hurts. But I realized He was right.

That was my first introduction to this year's "Topic for Growth." That's another way of saying the Lord doesn't let me get very far from this idea and its implications for me without sounding a warning bell. The subject: Obedience. Hour-by-hour obedience. It probably doesn't sound nearly so stimulating as it is actually turning out to be. It really is kind of exciting. I go ahead and make my plans, and God goes ahead and interrupts them. But I don't mind. Sometimes He sees things that need immediate attention that I don't know anything about, and therefore could obviously not plan into my schedule. But God comes along and whispers, "Up and at 'em, Jane." And instead of arguing, I "up and at 'em." And it's terrific what great results can come from such spontaneous living.

One Sunday, I had just changed my clothes into something I could easily relax in, when the Lord suggested I visit a girl I had met in a city-wide crusade. I said, "But Lord, I've just changed my clothes." No reply. Hmmm. So I changed my clothes again and proceeded to try and track her down. I went to the YWCA but she had moved. I finally found her place but she wasn't home. I left a note. She came to church that night. She and her friend went to the altar. I was mighty glad I hadn't argued about changing my clothes. And when God prompts me to write a letter to someone, I try always to sandwich it in with the other scheduled letters as well. You know something? God has a great sense of timing.

One last thing about this obedience stuff. It is based on His wisdom, not ours. So the instructions you may be asked to obey may not satisfy the fine points of your own reasoning powers. On the contrary, sometimes the requests may seem a bit unreasonable. But "ours is not to reason why."

One day recently, God whispered a quiet little directive in my ear that about knocked me off my feet. I've been going to school so many years I feel like a talking textbook. But here was God suggesting I do more studying yet, in the direction of ordination into the ministry. Now I wouldn't exactly say I ever argue with God, but we do occasionally have these "friendly discussions." After two days of airing my views, I hadn't swayed Him one bit. He can be awfully set in His ways at times!

He wasn't at all impressed with the many excellent reasons I gave for shelving the idea. Foremost, there seemed no time available for a home study course in my already loaded schedule. I couldn't imagine what folks would think. Besides, I've never been really too keen on women in the ministry, so how could I join their ranks? On top of that, I was thinking, I told everyone at home I was going to be a missionary forever. Now I'm here, and I like being a missionary, so why can't I just be a missionary forever? Life used to be so simple!

I pushed for more information. But He didn't seem to feel moved to explain to me in any further detail. "Does this mean I'm leaving the mission field? But I'm just learning the language! What did You have in mind? Evangelism? Missions conferences? The ministry proper?" Silence. Then: "Jane, just get the training." Obedience, just hour by hour, huh? "Okay Lord, I'll get it."

You know, God wasn't angry at me because my knees were quaking; He just stood patiently by while I got used to the idea. I realized that whatever He intends, His motivation is love for people. I don't want my motivation to be anything less. God needs each of us ready for whatever comes, assured that *all* things work out together for good to those who love the Lord and are the called according to His purposes.

11

Frog Grody Klutzit

Now I can just believe that a lot of you, especially the ones who know me, feel fairly aghast after reading this little book. "She's sure got her nerve to write such things! What does she mean by preaching at us that way? She's no better than the rest of us."

All I can say to that is, "Ain't it the truth!" I am so far from arriving that some people, I'm sure, doubt I ever left. I have my depressions, I make my mistakes, and otherwise generally "come short of the glory of God." But God loves me. Not just when my best foot's forward but all the time. I agree He no doubt prefers that I try to keep that good foot in front, but His love is sure, regardless. And, because God accepts me, I am just now learning to accept myself.

Curious about that Frog Grody Klutzit? That was my secret name for myself (until now that I've revealed it). I didn't get it all at once; it has taken years of hard effort to make the blunders that somehow make each of the names appropriate. It was a game I started. I can't even remember when. I use Frog Grody Klutzit to address myself when I do something bad. I use it to puncture the balloon when I notice I seem to be getting a bit "puffed up" about something. Invariably it puts me back in perspective. It recalls things to my mind—things characteristic of me, like parking tickets, spilled offering plates, and falls down stairs. Then there are the numerous occasions I have said things that were just plain dumb.

However, it is the *big* mistakes that really take the toll. I remember this one patient in particular who died. A nurse doesn't very often get taken by surprise when one of her patients dies. It doesn't take much experience to get this built-in sixth sense that says, "This patient is not good. Beware!" And with high-risk patients you just naturally keep an eye open. But one evening I had a 35-year-old father who was charging around and laughing just die on me. A cardiac arrest. Bingo and that was it. Resuscitation was tried but to no avail. All I could think was I had lost that father of four.

Unfortunately it wasn't the last time. I've lost many other patients through the years—that's part of working in a hospital. As most of them were carried away, I had a clear conscience that everything possible had been done for them. But there are those distinctive ones that always make you wonder, Could I have done something more? Maybe, just maybe, if I had known a bit more or seen my difficulties a little bit farther ahead, I could have saved the patient. Only God knows. But I tell you very sincerely that such things weigh heavy on the hearts of physicians and nurses. I love being a nurse when my patients recover, but I just don't get any charge out of fixing a shroud.

After one such occasion, I went around pointing a finger at myself for a few hours, until the Lord took me aside. "Life and death are in My hands, Jane. Do the best you can and leave it at that. You don't have to be another Albert Schweitzer. I love you as you are." I wouldn't trade those words for a doctorate in nursing from the best university in the land.

Then there was the time I thought I would try to enliven the youth group at church but finally decided to throw in the towel and direct my attentions elsewhere. That was real failure. I should have been able to handle both myself and that situation much better than I did. And I sure shouldn't have quit so soon. But, seeing a few thunderclouds appear on the horizon, I sounded retreat. Am I proud? If I were an ostrich, I would have stuck my head in the sand. But God has forgiven me that as well and used it for many profitable hours on how I might improve my techniques for a next time. I have come to realize more and more that God isn't condemning us. He is standing by with counsel and advice to help us—and Band-Aids if necessary.

But, there is one other bigger perplexity that bothered me for many, many years. I felt that while God might not ask or even expect success in those other areas, there was one thing He *was* looking for. And I felt sure that my inability to consistently produce it was downgrading me in God's eyes. It was this: I thought surely if I had God's love in my heart and flowing out through me, then my interpersonal relationships with everybody I met, and especially Christians, ought to be great. I should have had more fantastic friendships than a dog has fleas. But I didn't.

I am in no wise saying that Christians should find themselves at sword tips with one another. Something is *badly* wrong when that happens. But I am saying that not every Christian will be falling over backwards with infatuation for every other Christian.

People are different. Individuals see things from various vantage points. They have different personal histories behind them. Barnabas and Paul each saw Mark in a different light. Both were good Christian men, but they felt differently about him. It doesn't mean they sinned or yelled foul words over their backs at each other as they parted. It was simply a recognition of the fact that differences can exist and must be coped with. Before they chose to go their separate ways, they talked together. Then they did what they felt was right.

Not everyone at church is going to understand you. At least I'm sure they don't all understand me. Some will. And down through the years God will lead you to the fellowship of some who really "talk your language." Don't lose contact with these people. Write or phone, visit if you can, but keep those lines of communication open. No man is an island.

The main thing in life is that you must be true to God regardless of what the other fellow thinks or does. We worship God and not our fellowman, or our country, or even our church. God must have our first allegiance. Spend a lot of time with God and He will help you find out who you really are. If you are feeling tired and troubled, don't just take a vacation. Take a few days (whether you have time or not) and spend them entirely with God. He'll sort you out. It may not be in the manner you anticipate, but He'll get the job done anyway.

I have on many occasions been called a loner, and I can't deny that I am. My background has been such that I've always had to spend a lot of time alone. And, especially after I began to really get to know God, I didn't particularly mind it. For me, happiness is walking the fields of a farm, blazing a trail into the back country on my Honda, or discovering a waterfall in the woods. I feel very close to God in the outdoors. And lying on my bed reading His Word can take me to His feet at any time.

I used to try so hard to be whatever other people seemed to want me to be. And yet I'm not really me at a formal dinner or chatting away to a host of ladies at the garden club. No, if you want to know the real me, then look under the willow by the (dare I say?) old mill stream. I want to share my hideaways with you. There is no "Keep

103

Out" sign. But when you find me, let's not talk about the weather or our bunions, let's talk about God. I love Him so! You know what? God loves me too, even if I'm not the most sociable person in the world.

So you don't think Frog Grody Klutzit is anything special? Well, you're wrong. I *am* special. I'm special to God. And nobody could take a very close look at my life and the intensive care God has given it and deny that I'm special to God. I am!

But, SO ARE YOU! God doesn't have any favorites. He sees everybody in the same light. It's just that God thinks we are ALL special! He hasn't done anything for me He won't be glad to do for you. God's ready to shower each of us with His abundant affection. What more could He do to prove it to you than giving His Son to die on the Cross?

So you're feeling lonely? And your problems are getting you down? Are you looking for a friend to help you? How about that! All this time God has been looking for *you!*